Sweet Cane

Dr. Ariel Sylvester, Ed.D.

Pretty Nerd Publishing

Disclaimer: This book is a work of fiction, and the views expressed herein are the sole responsibility of the author. Likewise, certain characters, places, and incidents are the product of the author's imagination, and any resemblance to actual persons, living or dead, or actual events, is entirely coincidental.

Hardcover ISBN: 978-1-958240-16-8
Paperback ISBN: 978-1-958240-28-1
Ebook ISBN: 978-1-958240-04-5

Library of Congress Control Number: 2022907244

First paperback edition September 2022

Edited by Winter Murray at the DePaul Writing Center

Book design by Dr. Ariel Sylvester, Ed.D.

Cover art retrieved from http://unsplash.com

Layout by Dr. Ariel Sylvester, Ed.D.

Pretty Nerd Publishing
2220 W. Maypole Ave
Chicago, IL 60612
http://prettynerdpublishing.com

Printed in the United States of America

Table of Contents

Part 1: The Story of Andrea Kane

Chapter 1 - The Homicide

Police and ambulance sirens rang, yellow tape was hung, spectators were standing around in shock, and Detectives Stevenson and Williams were walking through the front entrance of a construction site of a high-rise condo building in Chicago. This 30-something, Black male and female Detective duo strutted onto the crime scene with their heads held high, shoulders squared, and guns on their hips. Detective Williams was wearing a suit as always. No matter how gruesome the crime scene was, this 6'5 chocolate-skinned, bearded man with locs down his back always looked as if he was posing for GQ magazine. Detective Stevenson on the other hand, always wore an uncoordinated button-down shirt, blazer, slacks, and loafers. She kept her hair cut short in a teenie-weenie afro, and wore the slightest touch of mascara and rose colored lipstick to compliment her mocha complexion. Although stunning with model-like facial features and a curvaceous body, she tried hard to mask her beauty with rage, courage, and strength to be taken seriously as a 5’7 Black, female detective. Thirty minutes before their arrival a construction worker had found a dead body buried underneath ten heavy bags of concrete mix. As the construction worker led the detectives to the dead body he frantically shared the story of how he came across it.

“I found the body here. My crew and I smelled a faint, foul smell in this area. We thought maybe it was a dead cat or rat. We started picking up the bags of concrete and we found the body of a young woman.”

“And you just now found her body and called 911?” Detective Stevenson asked.

“Yes, we haven’t been working on this site for a couple of weeks now. The owner of our construction company was dealing with some legal stuff so we couldn’t work until it was taken care of. This was our first day back on the job and we found the dead body.”

“Did the bags of concrete mix fall down from anywhere?” Detective Williams asked looking around.

“No, we keep the bags of concrete mix on the ground.” The construction worker was puzzled.

“I'm just wondering how this happened because I don't see any blood on the ground. I'm trying to see if she was crushed by the bags.”

“Yeah I don't see any blood either. Did you all see any blood anywhere when you entered the site?” Detective Stevenson asked.

“No, nothing. There was no blood anywhere,” the construction worker responded.

“Okay, we’ll have our people look around to see if there is any blood anywhere,” Detective Stevenson assured the construction worker.

“Did any of your crew recognize this girl?” Detective Williams asked.

“No, none of us. Nobody knew her, and after we moved the bags of concrete and saw her face nobody touched her.”

“So there is no blood, nobody knew her, nobody touched her, and yet she’s at this construction site? There are plenty of construction sites in Chicago, why is her dead body at this one?” Detective Williams asked

“I don’t know.” The construction worker shrugged.

"Okay, thank you sir," Detective Stevenson said.

"It's a shame, why would someone kill this girl? She looks to be the age of my own daughter. I mean, what did she do?" the construction worker asked.

"That's what we're going to try and find out," Detective Williams responded as he and Detective Stevenson walked away.

"You think he's telling the truth?" Detective Stevenson asked Detective Williams as they walked outside.

"About not being on the construction site for two weeks? Well someone was on the construction site. They buried the girl here."

"Not that. Do you think no one at this site knows this girl? Why would someone bury this girl here under bags of concrete mix? That doesn't seem like an accident. Why not throw her in the trash? Or throw her in Lake Michigan? Or bury her under dirt? Why bury her here, at this site?"

"Yeah, it doesn't seem random. I have a feeling we'll be going on a long journey to figure out who this girl is and who killed her."

"There they are," the detectives heard a construction worker yell as the stood outside the construction site.

“Hey tell them to let me through," a man commanded standing behind the yellow tape.

“Officer Cannon, who is this?" Detective Stevenson asked one of the officers holding the man back behind the yellow tape.

“I'm the boss. I'm the president of this construction company, the number one construction company in Chicago. I'm Nicholas Wright.”

“Okay, let him through," Detective Williams told the officer.

“What's going on? Did someone get hurt on the job?” Nicholas Wright asked. “My guys called me and said the police were here.”

“No, Mr. Wright. I'm Detective Williams, and this is Detective Stevenson. There was a dead body found at this construction site, and one of your workers reported it.”

“There was a dead body found on my construction site? Was it one of my workers? Did any of my workers know who it was?”

“No, they said they didn't, sir. It wasn’t one of the workers, it was the body of a young woman," Detective Stevenson assured him.

“Oh God. Well how did she die? Was she homeless or something? Did she sneak in here? My guys and I haven’t been at this site for a couple weeks now.”

“We don't know yet, sir, but I'm going to have to give you a heads up. This construction site is a crime scene," Detective Williams said.

“So what does that mean?" Nicholas Wright asked.

“Sir, one of your construction workers informed us already that they haven't been working for a couple weeks because you were dealing with some legal issues.”

“Yeah, so?”

“So you may have to push the timeline for this project back some more because we have to investigate this crime scene,” Detective Stevenson responded.

“How much of a push are we talking about?”

“We don't know yet.”

“Well can't you find out?”

“Sir we'll keep you posted, but until further notice you'll have to let your workers know that the project is off,” Detective Williams said, sensing Nicholas Wright’s hostility.

“What if this investigation takes too long and the people I'm doing business with decide to go with another company? That means I don't get my money and I don't get to put it in my worker's pockets.

These guys have already been on unpaid leave for two weeks," he responded, enraged.

"I understand that, sir. We'll figure this out as fast as we can," Detective Stevenson assured him as she and Detective Williams walked away from the construction site and Nicholas Wright was escorted back behind the yellow tape again.

"You still think it was one of the construction workers? I'm sure they knew that if a dead body was found, they would be out of work longer," Detective Williams said as the two detectives entered the car and drove to the medical examiner's office.

"I don't know, but whoever it was, this murder was planned. No blood anywhere, and the girl was buried but still visible enough to be found. I know they haven't been working for two weeks, but whoever did this knew that this body would be found eventually. They weren't trying to dispose of it. Let's get her to Coroner Burgess so he can perform the autopsy," Detective Stevenson responded.

"So Burgess, what did your autopsy reveal?" Detective Stevenson asked the coroner performing the autopsy at the medical examiner's office.

"Looking over this girl's body, she looks to be very young. She has been dead for over a week. She was shot four times in the chest by a shotgun, and that was her cause of death," Coroner Burgess responded as he pointed to gunshot wounds on the corpse.

"Okay, but I'm confused — she was shot, but there was no blood anywhere at the scene?"

"Well that's because her body was frozen after she was shot. I can tell by her autopsy."

"So she was shot and then frozen?"

"Yes, and then buried underneath the bags of concrete mix. Plus it's winter time here in Chicago, and it's been bitter cold days and extremely cold nights these past couple of weeks. So her body could've frozen because of the weather or could've been frozen before she was buried."

"Wow! Thanks, Burgess."

"There are also a few bruises on her back, arms, and chest. They don't look to be the size of a fist, so this could've happened if her body was moved. I also performed a rape kit on her, but I didn't find anything. That doesn't mean that it didn't happen; since the body was frozen it would be hard to detect. We didn't find any other DNA on her."

"Did she have anything on her? Any items or something?"

"No, I haven't found anything in her pockets, bra, nothing. Did you find out who this girl is?"

"Williams is looking into that now back at the police station. We have to contact her family to identify the body. If she has any family."

"Oh?" Coroner Burgess looked confused.

"I'll explain later. Williams will be upset if I don't talk to him about everything first. You know he's a baby about these things," Detective Stevenson joked as Coroner Burgess laughed.

"Well I'm just glad you finally have a partner that you get along with."

"You're glad? I'm glad, Williams has been the partner from detective heaven."

"Well you deserve it. You've had a few bad apples, but you ended up with a good one in the end."

"Thanks, and I'll let Williams know you feel that way. I'd never admit to him that he's that great. Later, Burgess." Detective Stevenson left the coroner's office to inform Detective Williams about the autopsy. As she drove a few blocks back to the police station, she hoped Detective Williams would have more information about the homicide visit.

“Williams, the autopsy report came back,” Detective Stevenson said as she walked up to Detective Williams’ desk inside of the police station.

“Okay, so what did we find? What’s the cause of death?”

“Burgess conducted the autopsy and found that our murder victim was shot four times in the chest by a shotgun. Judging by the autopsy, she's been dead for over a week now. Knowing that she was shot with a shotgun, I’d say it was domestic. A man had to kill her because women don’t usually shoot other women, and women don’t usually own shotguns. Especially not here in Chicago.”

“True, this does seem domestic. But we didn’t see any blood at the site. And she’s been dead for over a week, but the odor wasn’t that foul.”

“I know, so she wasn’t shot at the construction site. Her body had to be transported, which also makes me think this is domestic because a woman wouldn’t be able to move another woman’s dead body to a construction site without dragging it. There would be blood somewhere. Burgess didn’t say anything about dragging. There were also bruises on her body, according to the autopsy. And Burgess said that the body did seem to be frozen and thawed,” Detective Stevenson smiled.

“Yeah, definitely seems domestic and we’re definitely looking for a man. Well, our victim could've fought her killer or could've been bruised during the transport. And the freezing explains why there was no blood and the body didn’t smell that bad. Still doesn’t explain why she was at this particular construction site. But I'm confused as to why you're smiling? All this just makes our job more complicated.”

“I know, I think that’s exciting. Why be a detective if you’re not into a little bit of mystery?”

“Whatever, Stevie,” Detective Williams responded.

“So who is our victim?” Detective Stevenson asked.

“Her name is Andrea Kane, a 20-year-old White female from Chicago. No children, no spouse.”

“Does she have any relatives?”

“Well, she was in and out of her mother's care when she was younger. Mom, Alexis Kane, was deemed unfit and negligent, and she was abusing drugs. No status on her whereabouts, no address listed for her. She's still alive, but there is no telling where she is. Eventually Andrea and her little sister, Emily Kane, moved in with their grandmother, Emilia Kane, when Andrea was 10. Grandmother died when Andrea was 16. She and Emily moved in with Ms. Kimberly Baker. She's been their foster mother for these past few years."

"So she's a foster kid. They usually have a run-in with the law at some point. Is there anything on her record?" Detective Stevenson walked over to Detective Stevenson's computer to read what was on the screen.

"Oh yeah, there was a DUI last year and driving with an expired license. There was an assault by her that was reported a couple years ago. There was a theft when she was a minor. And she had a few shoplifting incidents as a minor."

"So nothing major, except for that assault. Let's look into that assault. Who was it reported by and who was it done on?" Detective Stevenson asked as she went to her computer. "It was reported by a male named Austin Clay, and he was also the victim."

"You think Austin had something to do with her death? Maybe he's a boyfriend? We just confirmed that this does seem like a domestic homicide," Detective Williams asked.

“I don't think so. According to our records Austin Clay doesn't live in Chicago. He lives in Texas.”

“Let me guess, in Austin?”

“Ding. Ding. Ding. You got it! They were at a bar when she assaulted him.”

“But that doesn't mean he wasn't here when the murder happened,” Detective Williams responded, throwing paper balls in the garbage.

“I know, but why would he just leave her body there like that?”

“I don't know, that’s the part that’s not making any sense. So how old is Emily Kane, the sister? She seems to be the next of kin”

“Emily Kane just turned 18 last month.”

“Is she still with the foster mother?”

“I don't know, it says she might be. But since she just turned 18, her residence could not be updated in the system.”

“Well, before we go after this Austin Clay, we gotta tell the foster mom since there is no telling where the real mom is. Then we gotta see where the sister is and tell her.”

“Yeah, and maybe both of them can prove that you're wrong and I'm right, and that Austin Clay didn't do it.”

“Yeah, yeah, yeah, are you heading home?” Detective Williams rolled his eyes and put his coat on.

“No, I'm going to look into this more. Maybe I can find some more suspects or something by looking at her social media accounts.”

"Look overachiever, don't stay here too late. We'll pay a visit to the foster mother tomorrow.”

“Okay, tell Cheryl I said hello.”

“I will. She's making chili tomorrow. Do you want me to bring you some?”

“Actually I'll stop by and eat with you all, if that's okay.”

“Sure, my wife would like that. I'll let her know,” Detective Williams smiled.

“Alright, see you tomorrow,” Detective Stevenson said while glaring at the computer.

“See you, Stevie. Get some sleep, we have important things to do tomorrow.”

The next morning at 9:00 am, the detectives were driving on their way to visit the old foster mother’s house to get answers about Emily and Andrea Kane.

“So the newscaster reported that a body was found at the construction site, but they didn’t say who?” Detective Stevenson asked.

“Yeah, the chief told me we need to reach out to the relatives today so that they can identify the body. Then he’s going to have to make a statement to the media about the girl and her cause of death,” Detective Williams responded.

“Well I looked at her social media pages last night. She was a beautiful young lady; looking at her dead body lying there dead you wouldn’t be able to tell,” Detective Stevenson said.

“Really?”

“Yeah, and she looked to be living a lavish life. She had pictures of watches, nice cars, nice handbags and shoes, diamonds, a nice place, and nice trips across the world.”

“Really? How does a 20 year old who used to be a foster kid afford all of that? Is she an influencer, as those young kids call it nowadays?”

“I don’t think so. Influencers usually have sponsored content on their social media platforms, and she didn’t show that anything was sponsored.”

"So do you think she might've stolen these items or obtained them fraudulently?"

"I don't know, but all of the lavish stuff didn't line up with who she was. A foster kid who has a negligent, drug-abusing mother and an absentee father, grew up with her grandmother, and now all of a sudden at 20 she's living this lavish life? It doesn't make sense. I also couldn't tell her occupation from her social media, either."

"Did she say anything about feeling like she was in some kind of trouble on her social media sites?"

"Not from what I saw. Even when I looked back through her timeline I didn't see anything. But she did have pictures with the foster mom, Ms. Kimberly Baker, and the sister, Emily Kane. She had a picture from Emily's birthday with the caption 'mom and sis.'"

"Okay, so we seem to have the right girl. Maybe the sister is still with the foster mother."

"Yeah, maybe." Detective Stevenson stared out the passenger side window confused.

"You still seem like you're trying to piece it together."

"I am. I hope the foster mother will be able to give us some information."

"Well, did she mention anything about Austin Clay?"

"No, I didn't see anything about him. I'm telling you, he's not a suspect," Detective Stevenson smiled.

"Okay, okay. Well let's see what the foster mother has to say." Detective Williams parked in front of the old foster mother's house. They exited their car and stepped onto her porch.

Knock. Knock. Knock.

"Who is it?" what sounded like the voice of a child asked from behind the door.

"Hi, this is Detective Stevenson and Detective Williams, we're looking for Ms. Kimberly Baker. Is she here?"

"Mama Kim, there are detectives at the door for you," the child yelled out. Ms. Kimberly Baker answered the door, looking concerned.

"Hello, I'm Ms. Kimberly Baker, is something wrong?" A plump, middle-aged, short White woman with gray hair and glasses answered the door.

"Ma'am, we have some news about Andrea Kane. Can we please come in?" Detective Williams asked.

“Yes, but I would like to inform you that Andrea Kane isn’t under my custody anymore,” Ms. Kimberly Baker stood behind the screen door as two children who looked to be the ages of ten and twelve stood behind her.

“We know, ma’am, we still would like to tell you the news we have,” Detective Stevenson said. Ms. Kimberly Baker could tell by the detective's eyes that something was wrong so she opened the door and allowed them in.

“Please have a seat at my dining table here in the kitchen. I’m sorry, I wasn’t expecting anyone, so the children’s toys are everywhere. Would you both like something to drink?”

“No ma’am, but thank you for offering us refreshments, and don’t worry about the children’s toys. I’m a father myself, so I understand,” Detective Williams said with a smile on his face that seemed to calm Ms. Kimberly Baker’s nerves.

“Yes Ms. Baker, we're not here about the children. In fact, we know that you have been a foster mother for many years and have high approval ratings from child protective services,” Detective Stevenson said as the children walked up to Ms. Kimberly Baker to hug her.

"Thank you, Detective. Children, why don't you go to your rooms to play. I'll make you a snack while I talk to these nice people."

"Okay, Mama Kim," the children said as they ran off to their rooms together.

"Are these your only foster children, ma'am?" Detective Williams asked.

"For now, yes. I've had Maya and Sadie for a few months now. I've been a foster mother for eleven years. So even though it's Maya and Sadie now, I could house more children in a couple months."

"What made you want to become a foster mother?" Detective Stevenson asked.

"I was a teacher for several years. I could never have children of my own. My husband at the time didn't want to adopt and blamed me for not giving him a lineage. So when he left me, I decided to become a foster mother. I had been taking care of children as a teacher, a mentor, and babysitter, so I felt that becoming a foster mother was my next thing." Ms. Kimberly Baker prepared the children a snack from the fridge.

"That's very noble of you, ma'am," Detective Williams said, smiling.

"Thank you. I enjoy being a foster mother. Some of the kids stay for a while, and some come back around when they're old enough. Even if they don't stay, being able to help children and their parents until they're reunited is amazing. I wasn't able to have kids of my own, so now after becoming a foster mother, I have a lot of children." Ms. Kimberly Baker looked at the detectives' faces. "Andrea Kane was one of those children who stuck around. When their grandmother passed away, she and Emily came to stay with me. Usually foster children stay for two years and then leave. Andrea was sixteen going on seventeen when she came, and she moved out once she turned eighteen. She got into a bit of trouble while she was here, but me and Child Protective Services understood.

Andrea had gone through a lot, being the oldest. Their mother was on drugs; she would leave them home sometimes, leaving Andrea and Emily to fend for themselves. She was abusive, and she even allowed a man to abuse Andrea for drugs. Eventually one of Emily's teachers called Child Protective Services because Emily had bruises on her arm. They looked into their living conditions, started asking the children questions, and they placed them in their grandmother's care. Once their grandmother passed away, they were placed into foster care, and that's when they ended up with me. I didn't have any other children at the time, and Child Protective Services didn't want to separate them. They placed them with me because they knew I wouldn't mind taking care of both of them. Andrea was a tough nut to crack, but eventually she came around. Emily was always sweet."

"Thank you for sharing that. Did Andrea ever talk to you about her mother and where she might be now?" Detective Williams asked.

"No, they haven't seen their mother since she came to their grandmother's door-step asking for money to buy drugs. Andrea was fourteen at the time."

"Does Emily still live with you?" Detective Stevenson asked. "We saw that she turned eighteen last month."

"No, Andrea got an apartment last year when she was 19 and Emily was 17. Emily had been with me for two years, and Child Protective Services was talking about putting her in another foster home. That's when she started to fight for emancipation, and when it was granted, she moved in with Andrea. The girls have been living together for about a year now."

"Do you know where they live now, ma'am?" Detective Williams asked.

"Yes, I helped them decorate their apartment. Even though Emily was emancipated and Andrea moved out, they still call me their mother. They told me their grandmother was their mother who died, their biological mother was their mother who hurt them, and I was their mother that they still had. So they call me Mama Kim. That's why Maya and Sadie call me Mama Kim now. Andrea and Emily came over for Emily's birthday last month. I made her a cake, and Andrea bought gifts for me, the kids, and Emily. She gave me this bracelet." Ms. Kimberly Baker showed off her diamond bracelet.

"Yeah, we were looking on Andrea's social media, and we saw that she lived a very lavish life? Do you know what she did for a living?" Detective Williams asked.

"She told me she got a job as a flight attendant. She was always going on trips and showing me pictures. I asked her why she spent her money on so many lavish gifts. She told me that she wanted to give herself and Emily the life their mother couldn't and didn't give them. And she wanted to thank me for loving them and taking care of them. She also told me she wished she could've given more to their grandmother before she passed away." Ms. Kimberly Baker paused mid-conversation. “Detectives, is Andrea missing?” She stood with her hands on the counter, looking out the kitchen window in dismay.

“No ma’am. I don’t know how to tell you this. I hear the way you talk about Andrea, and I can tell you really love her and Emily. We know that you’re basically their mother, so we wanted to ask you…” Detective Stevenson began to say before Ms. Kimberly Baker cut her off.

“Just come out and say it, Detective.” Ms. Kimberly Baker looked at the detective with tears in her eyes.

“We found a dead body at the construction site of a high-rise condo building,” Detective Stevenson began to say as Ms. Kimberly Baker began to cry and Detective Williams came up to her to hug her. “We have reason to believe that the victim was Andrea Kane.”

“I’m so sorry. I just can’t believe this. Have you told Emily?” Ms. Kimberly Baker asked through her tears. “She’s her next of kin.”

“No, we came here to find out Emily’s whereabouts and thought maybe she was still here,” Detective Stevenson said.

“Emily takes classes at one of the community colleges here in Chicago. She also does work study, but she should be home now.” Ms. Kimberly Baker kept crying.

“I’m sorry, Ms. Baker,” Detective Williams said as he was still hugging her.

“How did she die?” Ms. Kimberly Baker asked.

“I think we should wait until we talk to Emily,” Detective Stevenson began to say. “Since she’s her next of kin.”

“Okay,” Ms. Kimberly Baker responded through her tears.

“When she goes to identify the body we’ll tell her to call you,” Detective Williams said.

“Wait, I don’t want her to find out alone. I want to show her that I’m here for her. Can I call her to come over, please?”

“Sure, ma’am, if that’ll lighten the blow. Andrea and Emily sound as if they’ve been through enough already,” Detective Stevenson said. Afterwards, Ms. Kimberly Baker dialed Emily’s number. She gained as much composure as she could to talk to Emily without crying.

“Emily? Hi sweetheart, how are you?” Ms. Kimberly Baker asked Emily after she answered. “Listen, Emily, I have something I need to tell you. Could you please come over right away?” Ms. Kimberly Baker wiped her tears. “Yes, sweetheart, I need you to come over right away.” The detectives sat at the table, looking at her.

About thirty minutes later, Emily Kane arrived at Ms. Kimberly Baker's house. She knocked on the door, and Ms. Kimberly Baker answered.

"Hey Mama Kim!" Emily said as she came in and hugged Ms. Kimberly Baker. The detectives looked at one another dismally. Emily was in good spirits, and they knew their announcement was about to change that.

"Hi Emily, how are you, my dear?" Ms. Kimberly Baker asked as Emily walked in.

"I'm good, Mama Kim." Emily stopped walking and talking as she saw the detectives standing in Ms. Kimberly Baker's living room. "Mama Kim, what's going on? Who are these people?"

"Hi Emily, I'm Detective Stevenson, and this is Detective Williams. We have some unfavorable news…"

"Wait, Mama Kim, are they here about the kids? Mama Kim is the best foster mother…" Emily interrupted.

"They're not here about the kids, Emily, they're here about Andrea," Ms. Kimberly Baker said, grabbing Emily's hand.

"Wait, why would they be here about Andrea?" Emily asked, confused.

"Andrea… Andrea is…" Ms. Kimberly Baker responded as she cried.

"What's wrong with Andrea, Mama Kim?" Emily asked as she placed her hands on Ms. Kimberly Baker's shoulders.

"We have reason to believe that your sister, Andrea, was found dead at the construction site of a high-rise condo building here in Chicago. We were coming here so that you can identify the body. I'm really sorry, Emily," Detective Stevenson said as Emily just stood there in shock. She didn't cry, she didn't say anything, she just stood there staring at the detectives in disbelief.

"You… you said Andrea is dead?" she finally uttered.

"We believe so, we need you to identify the body since you're her next of kin," Detective Stevenson responded.

"Okay. Okay, um… let's go," Emily turned around slowly and headed for the door as the detectives followed behind her. They looked at each other as if to say, "What's going on?" They were shocked by her response. Emily stood outside on Ms. Kimberly Baker's porch, waiting for the detectives to tell her what to do next.

"Ms. Baker, after Emily identifies the body, we'll have her tell you our next stops to find out who did this to Andrea and the news announcements," Detective Stevenson said.

"Do you think I should go too? Should I leave the kids with a neighbor?" Ms. Kimberly Baker asked as she and the detectives came out onto the front porch with Emily.

"No, Mama Kim, no. I'll come back and tell you what happened," Emily said. "Should I drive in my car, or will you all take me?" she asked with her head down and her eyes staring at the ground as the detectives and Ms. Kimberly Baker all looked at her stunned by her reaction.

"We can take you if you don't feel comfortable driving," Detective Williams responded finally.

"Okay," she said as she slowly walked down the porch stairs towards the detectives' car.

As the three of them drove to the medical examiner's office, no one uttered anything. Emily sat in the back of the car looking dazed and confused. There were still no tears in her eyes. Instead of looking out the window, she kept her head down and looked at the floor. Detective Stevenson sat silently, wondering if she should say anything. She glanced over at Detective Williams for reassurance, and he shook his head to tell her not to ask Emily any questions right now. When they finally arrived at the coroner to identify the body, Emily still had the same look on her face as they walked into the building. She was walking with her arms folded, not speaking, and not looking at anyone. They entered Coroner Burgess' autopsy room, and he pulled Andrea Kane's body out of a wall that housed many other people's dead loved ones.

"Emily, is this your sister, Andrea Kane?" Detective Stevenson asked her softly.

Emily looked at the corpse's face. It was pale, bruised, and a bit bloody, but it looked to be her sister. Then she looked at the corpse's wrist. Emily and Andrea had recently gotten matching tattoos for Emily's birthday last month when she turned eighteen. After she saw this tattoo, she cried and wailed loudly. She began to fall to the ground, and as she did, Detective Williams tried to hold her up. The detectives and Coroner Burgess could tell by Emily's reaction that this was her sister, Andrea Kane.

“Okay, you can close it, Burgess,” Detective Stevenson told the coroner as Emily was still wailing loudly in Detective Williams’ arms. Coroner Burgess closed the case that housed the dead Andrea Kane.

“I need to sit down. I need to sit down,” Emily said through her wailing.

“Of course,” Detective Williams said as he walked with Emily to the car so they could take her back to the police station for questioning. This time, Emily cried in the back seat of the detective’s car. Instead of looking down, she leaned her head on the backseat window. Once the detectives arrived at the police station, they walked Emily into an interrogation room to have a seat, a drink of water, and a moment to process everything. She cried silently inside the interrogation room. The detectives entered the other side of the one-way glass. They looked through the window and saw Emily sitting in shock. Tears streamed down her face, but no sound came out of her mouth. She hadn’t touched her water, and she continuously wiped her nose with her sleeve. She sat with her head hanging down and her hair covering most of her face. A heartbreaking and lonely sight to the detectives.

“So do you think we should call Ms. Baker to come and get her?” Detective Williams asked.

“We have to tell her how Andrea died, maybe she knows something,” Detective Stevenson said.

“I know, but look at her. How is she going to process all of that? She’s only eighteen.”

“I know, but we have a job to do. Did you see her face when we told her about Andrea at Ms. Baker’s house? She looked like she had seen a ghost.”

“Yeah, I noticed. Maybe a small piece of her hoped that it wasn’t her sister.”

“Hey, we never asked either of them the last time they talked to Andrea. Andrea has been dead for over a week, and they never reported her missing?”

“Already ahead of you, that’s why I placed her in here for questioning. Her reaction at Ms. Baker’s house along with neither of them saying the last time they spoke with Andrea just didn’t sit right with me. Also, did you catch that Ms. Baker just assumed Andrea was missing? I wonder — why they didn’t report her missing, then?” Detective Williams said.

"Yeah, I did catch that. Alright let's head in," The detectives entered the room to question Emily.

"Alright Emily, we know this is a lot to take in, but we have to explain to you how your sister died," Detective Stevenson said as Emily sat with her head down. The detectives sat down across the table from her. "Are you ready?" Detective Stevenson asked as Emily nodded in agreement.

"Your sister, Andrea, was found dead at the construction site of a high-rise condo building in Chicago. She suffered four gunshot wounds to the abdomen, she was bruised, and she had been frozen, thawed, and transported. She was found by one of the construction workers underneath ten bags of concrete mix," Detective Williams said.

"We haven't been able to identify her killer yet, so we were hoping that you would be able to help us."

"We saw that she assaulted someone last year by the name Austin Clay. Has your sister seen him lately?" Detective Williams asked.

"Isn't that the guy who she punched at the bar last year?" Emily kept her head down as she wiped her nose and her tears with her sleeve.

"Yes, that's him," Detective Williams said.

"No, she hasn't seen him since then. She was bailed out the same night she was arrested. He never pressed charges for it, just reported it. He flirted with Andrea at the bar, and she wasn't interested. He wouldn't leave her alone, so she punched him in the face and kept punching him."

"How did your sister get inside the bar when she was still only 20?" Detective Williams asked.

"Fake I.D."

"Okay, never mind Austin Clay. Emily, you have to help us here. Did your sister ever say she was in any type of trouble?" Detective Stevenson asked.

"No, she didn't." Emily was still watching the floor, and tears kept streaming down her face.

"Well Ms. Baker told us your sister was a flight attendant…" Detective Williams began to say before Emily interrupted him.

"My sister wasn't a flight attendant."

"Well, why did Ms. Baker tell us that?" Detective Stevenson asked as her eyebrows lowered in confusion.

"Because that's what Andrea told Mama Kim she does for work. She didn't tell her the truth about how she makes her money."

"Well what does she do?" Detective Stevenson asked, but Emily didn't respond. The detectives looked at one another in frustration.

"Emily, when was the last time you spoke to your sister?" Detective Williams asked, but Emily didn't respond.

"Emily, you have to help us. We're trying to find out who killed your sister. There was no blood at the scene of the crime. There was no evidence. All of the construction workers said they never knew her and never met her. Your sister was shot and frozen. She hasn't seen Austin Clay since the bar fight. Now you're saying she wasn't a flight attendant. You have to give us some information so we can…" Detective Stevenson said before Emily interrupted.

"FINE." Emily banged her hands on the table loudly. She finally made eye contact with the detectives. They were startled by her reaction but showed no emotion. "Fine, my sister was not a flight attendant. She was a sugar baby. That's how she made her money."

"A sugar baby? What's that?" Detective Williams asked.

“A sugar baby is a young person who has a sugar mama or daddy, an older person who gives them money in return for sexual favors, company, time, stuff like that,” Detective Stevenson said.

“Yeah, exactly. My sister had three sugar daddies who would give her money. That’s how she’s been able to afford her lifestyle. I guess it all finally caught up to her,” Emily looked back down at the floor and wiped her nose with her sleeve.

“Emily, what do you mean by ‘it all finally caught up to her’?” Detective Stevenson asked.

“I mean her doing this sugar baby thing. I told her it was dangerous and that I didn’t agree with it. But Andrea has always been the pretty one of the two of us. I was always the smart one. All of my teachers talked to me about going to college because I was the smart one. They always pushed me to be better and had high expectations of me. Andrea’s teachers never told her she was smart, never pushed her, and didn’t expect anything from her. She didn’t do well in school, never paid attention, and she was always in trouble. Andrea wasn’t a bad person — we had just been through a lot, you know. Our mom was on drugs, our grandmother died, and we became foster kids. Andrea was always trying to look out for me and make sure I was okay, but because I was a good kid, everyone else looked out for me too. Not a lot of people looked out for her. I chose books. I chose to go to college because that's what everyone told me I should do since I was a great student. Andrea didn't choose that path. When she turned eighteen, she moved out of Mama Kim's place with some friends. They introduced her to this whole sugar baby lifestyle. She threw herself into it and had three sugar daddies."

"How was she able to do this?" Detective Williams asked.

"There are a few apps out there, right?" Detective Stevenson asked.

"Yeah, I guess. Anyway, when she started I told her to be careful. Eventually Andrea told Mama Kim that she wanted me to move in with her. Her sugar daddies would give her enough money for a place, a car, and clothes, and she could finally take care of me like she always wanted. She told Mama Kim that she was a flight attendant because she didn't want her to worry, and she didn't want her to judge her," Emily finished.

"Well that's a plot twist," Detective Williams said as he sat back in his chair, amazed.

“So you believe that maybe one of her sugar daddies did this to her?” Detective Stevenson asked. “I mean we believe that this is a domestic homicide. Her body wasn’t buried well, and someone could’ve easily found it. It was also transported and we believe only a man would’ve been able to transport the body”

“I mean, who else could it be? Either them or their wives or girlfriends because they ended up finding out about my sister. Maybe it was one of the men and their wife or girlfriend. In the words of William Congreve, ‘hell hath no fury like a woman scorned.’”

“So now our suspects could possibly be her three sugar daddies and their girlfriends or wives?” Detective Williams asked. “And we might be looking for two killers instead of one.”

“Emily, do you know who your sister’s sugar daddies were and how often she’d meet them?” Detective Stevenson asked.

“Of course. Andrea told me everything about her life as a sugar baby, the good and bad,” Emily responded, still looking down.

“Good, can you give us names?” Detective Stevenson asked.

“Nicholas Wright, Calvin Bruno, and Albert Little.”

“Wait, Nicholas Wright? That’s the name of the man who is the president of the construction company that’s working on the building where your sisters body was found,” Detective Stevenson said.

“When you said you found her at a construction site, I instantly thought of him,” Emily responded.

“Well then, he’s our first suspect,” Detective Williams said.

“Emily, we may need to keep you here a bit longer for questioning, if that’s okay?” Detective Stevenson asked, and Emily just shrugged her shoulders as she looked down at the floor. Both the detectives sat and looked at her and then each other. At that moment, they realized Emily wasn’t another family member of a homicide victim. She was a child who had just turned 18 and lost the one person in her life who she was closest to.

“Emily, if you want to go home or talk to Ms. Baker, you…” Detective Williams began to say.

“No, I want to find out who did this to my sister. So I’m willing to tell you everything about her and about me,” Emily responded abruptly with her head down.

“Okay then, well whenever you’re ready, we’re ready,” Detective Stevenson said.

"I'm guessing you all didn't find her phone when you found her body?" Emily asked rhetorically as she lifted her head to look at the detectives again.

"No, we didn't find her with any belongings, just her clothes," Detective Williams said

"How did you know that, Emily?" Detective Stevenson asked.

"Remember when you all asked me when was the last time I talked to my sister?"

"Yeah, the autopsy confirmed that Andrea has been dead for over a week. But neither you or Ms. Baker reported her dead or missing," Detective Stevenson asked.

"My sister texted me this morning, and I texted her back. She assured me that she was fine and that she was with one of her sugar daddies. That's why I needed to see her body to know that she was dead. Whoever killed my sister has been texting me from her phone, lying to me and making me believe that it was her. I had a funny feeling that she wasn't being honest; little did I know it wasn't her." The detectives now had that same look on their faces that Emily had when she was at Ms. Kimberly Baker's house. "I want to find the person who killed my sister, took her phone, lied to me, played games with me, and buried her at Nicholas Wright's construction site."

Chapter 2 - The Sister

Emily sat in the interrogation room, waiting for the detectives to question her about her phone, the text messages she's been receiving for the past week, and her sister's life as a sugar baby for the past couple of years. She sat thinking of her sister and the wonderful and horrible memories they'd shared. The horrible memories of their time with their biological mother. The horrible memories of their mother's friends who would come and get high with her. The horrible memories of their mom leaving them to fend for themselves. The horrible memories of sitting home for days, wondering if their mother was dead. The wonderful memories of time spent with their grandmother, the wonderful memories of finally having a stable, warm, loving home with food on the table. Emily and Andrea would always wonder how their horrible mother could come from such a wonderful person like their grandmother. When their grandmother died, their world came crashing down. They feared being split up and never seeing each other again. No matter how horrible life was with their mother, their world was wonderful because they were always together. But Child Protective Services had placed them with Mama Kim, and she had been the best foster mother they could have asked for. "*How could Andrea be gone?*" Emily thought to herself. *"How could I not realize that it wasn't her texting me?"* She thought again. With this last thought, the detectives walked in.

"So Emily, we would like to confiscate your phone as evidence for this case since you said your sister texted you this morning from her phone," Detective Stevenson said as Emily sat there staring down at the floor.

"With your statement, we have reason to believe that the person texting you from her phone could be someone you both knew," Detective Williams said.

"I don't want to give up my phone just yet. You all can get my phone records, but I don't want to give you my phone," Emily said with her head still down.

"Emily, we need it as evidence," Detective Stevenson said.

“I know what you’re saying, but you need me to cooperate for you all to find out who did this to my sister, right?” Emily responded, looking the detectives in the eyes now.

“Yes, Emily, your cooperation is needed to help in this investigation,” Detective Williams said.

“Okay, so I don’t want to give you my phone, but I’ll still cooperate and I’ll tell you everything you need to know,” Emily responded.

“Emily, it doesn't really work like that. Look, we know you’ve been through a lot…” Detective Stevenson began.

“No, no you don’t know what I’ve gone through. You have no idea what my sister and I have gone through…” Emily said through her tears as a look of anger appeared on her face. “You said you wanted me to tell you everything about Andrea and I. Before you confiscate my phone, let me tell you what I know.”

“Okay, that’s fine Emily, do that. Tell us everything we need to know so that we can find your sister’s killer,” Detective Williams said.

“Why don’t you want to give us the phone?” Detective Stevenson asked.

“Because I want to find out who did this to my sister…”

"That's our job, you don't need to worry about…" Detective Stevenson began to say before Emily abruptly interrupted her and banged on the table again.

"NO. No. Andrea was my sister. It's always been me and her. We cared for each other, we loved each other, we went through everything together. She's gone, and now I have no one. She was the person I looked up to. The person who protected me, and now she's gone. I want to help you figure out who murdered my sister. I don't want to give you my phone yet because I want to keep texting them. Maybe some way, somehow, I can find out who they are from these messages. Please give me that much. I have nothing else, just give me that much. Give me this chance to help you find out who my sister's killer is to avenge her death and give me some closure," Emily asked.

"Emily I don't know if we could do…" Detective Williams began to say.

"We can do that," Detective Stevenson said, interrupting Detective Williams.

"What?" Detective Williams asked.

"You can?" Emily said, looking up at the detectives now.

"Yes," Detective Stevenson said.

"No. Stevenson, how can we do that? We can't do that."

"Yes we can. We can get Emily's phone records. She can't be without her phone, right? And she can lead us towards the killer by texting them and pretending she doesn't know."

"What about the chief?" Detective Williams asked. "He won't be too happy with that."

"I know, and I'm willing to take the discipline that comes with this decision. I have a feeling these text messages could lead us to Andrea's killer. I'll have one of the officers find out when the last message was sent," Detective Stevenson said, smiling enthusiastically.

"Well I guess we're doing this then, Emily," Detective Williams said shaking his head.

"Thank you," Emily said, holding her head down again..

"So we'll get copies of your phone records, and you can keep texting the person who has your sister's phone. We will question her sugar daddies and potentially their wives and girlfriends. But there are stipulations. You have to be careful, Emily, and you can't text anything that we don't approve of. You can't schedule a meeting with this person without telling us first. If they stop responding to your texts at any point, let us know, especially after we bring her sugar daddies in for questioning. This could give us some information about who the killer is."

"Okay, I promise. I can send you guys screenshots of our phone conversations."

"No need; since your phone is evidence, we can attach our app and this chip to it so that the messages automatically come to our records," Detective Williams responded.

"Yeah, that way we can see it in real time." Detective Stevenson said.

"So you all are going to invade my privacy like Alexa, Siri, and Cortana, huh?"

"Well, you wanted to be a part of this investigation, so those are the rules." Detective Stevenson stared at Emily.

"Alright, I'm fine with that. Anything to find my sister's killer," Emily responded.

"Okay, so tell us more about you and your sister and her life as a sugar baby," Detective Stevenson said.

"Okay, um…can we order some pizza? I'm hungry."

"Uh…sure," Detective Williams said as both he and Detective Stevenson glanced at one another in amazement. "I'll place the order."

The pizza was now on the table. Emily had grabbed a slice and ate with her head down. Detective Williams and Stevenson each grabbed a slice too, but they stared at Emily as they ate.

"Alright Emily, pizza is here. Before we talk about the text messages, tell us about Andrea and her life as a sugar baby," Detective Stevenson said.

"Okay, um… Andrea started this whole sugar baby thing a couple years ago. She turned eighteen and could no longer stay with Mama Kim. Another sucky part of being a foster kid — you move around a lot, and you don't get to stay with one family. Anyway, she moved in with a friend from high school and a friend she met working at Walmart. The three of them decided to become roommates. They had a small, raggedy, two-bedroom apartment. Regardless, it was somewhere to stay. Since Andrea had to move out, I would go over there to be with her from time to time," Emily said between bites.

"What were the names of the girls she moved in with?" Detective Stevenson asked.

"Veronica Bridges and Riley Mensa. Veronica was a couple years older than Riley and Andrea, and the apartment was hers. She allowed both of them to come in as roommates once they graduated high school. She was the one who started being a sugar baby first. She came home with lavish gifts from her sugar daddy and told Riley and Dre about all the nice things he did for her. She would also tell them about what she had to do with him in order to get these things. This sounded good to Riley and Dre, and they decided to become sugar babies too." Emily placed her slice of pizza on the interrogation table. "When Andrea told me that she was going to become a sugar baby, I didn't approve. I thought it was dangerous and that Andrea could find another way to make money. She said, 'Em, what am I going to do? I'm not smart like you, I can't get through college.' I told her she could take up a trade, but she felt that she wouldn't get as much money."

"How did she feel when you didn't agree?" Detective Stevenson asked.

"She was upset, but she understood. She explained to me that she might as well try to make it off of her looks since that's all anyone ever told her she had or gave her attention for. Then she guilt-tripped me a bit. She started talking about the man that assaulted her when she was younger, all the guys that hit on her and slept with her but didn't truly want to be with her. She felt that by being a sugar baby, she would finally get something out of being with a man. She felt that she controlled everything this time. Everything was on her terms, there was no *real* relationship, and the sugar daddies would give her the things she always wanted out of it. In her mind, it was a win-win."

"But you still weren't comfortable with that?" Detective Stevenson said.

"No, I wasn't, but she was the big sister, not me. So she did what she wanted to do. I just wanted to watch out for her like she had always done for me. She told me not to tell Mama Kim because she would worry too much. For a while, she stayed with Veronica and Riley, and they would exchange creepy and kinky sugar daddy stories. Even though they were creepy, I never thought my sister would be murdered. Andrea's first sugar daddy was Nicholas Wright. He was president of a construction company, the number one construction company in Chicago. He had a wife and three kids. He told Andrea that he never told his wife he had a sugar baby. He would take Andrea out to dinner, he gave her a credit card to go shopping, and he helped her pay for her first car. She would text me whenever she would leave with him. I was always so worried about her. He eventually wanted to go on a trip with some of his male friends to Las Vegas, and he paid for Andrea to come. I was even more worried about her, but she kept texting me pictures and telling me she was having the time of her life. She told me that one day she would take me to Vegas too. She came back after a weekend, and I was happy to see her and to see that she was okay."

"So that's the story with Nicholas Wright. What about the other two, Calvin Bruno and Albert Little?" Detective Stevenson asked.

"Andrea decided that she wanted a second sugar daddy when things with Nicholas would slow down."

"What do you mean slow down?" Detective Williams asked.

"Well, Nicholas wasn't consistent. He would come around a bit, maybe a weekend, maybe for a couple of days. Then she wouldn't hear from him for months. He would send her money, but not as much as he would give her when they were together. Sometimes he wouldn't send her anything or wouldn't answer his phone. I guess because he was married with children, he had to tend to his duties as a husband and father. That's when she met Calvin Bruno. Calvin didn't have a wife or children, so he had more time to be with Andrea. He's a world-renowned psychologist. Talk about using your career for evil."

"What do you mean?" Detective Stevenson asked.

"He was an older man preying on younger women with issues. Not everyone realizes that young women like my sister have a lot of issues, but Calvin does because he's a psychologist. Calvin Bruno was my sister's second sugar daddy, and she thought he would have more time for her since he didn't have a wife and children, but he didn't. Calvin was surrounded by women. He was a good-looking doctor with tons of money to spend, and all the ladies flocked to him. After about six months of being with Calvin, Andrea looked at his social media and found out he had a young girlfriend. She didn't care about him having a girlfriend, she just wanted to make sure the girlfriend didn't take his time and money away from her."

"What was his girlfriend's name? Do you know?" Detective Williams said.

"After stalking her on social media, Andrea said her name was Lily Bostitch. She works for Google. Andrea asked Calvin how they met, and he told her the whole story. That's a big thing that was creepy to me about those guys, they loved talking about their significant others with my sister as if she was another dude." Emily shook her head.

“Did Lily know about Andrea?” Detective Stevenson asked.

“Not for a while. But then she saw a text message from Andrea to Calvin. She approached him about the messages. Calvin ended up seeing my sister and told her the whole story about how Lily was furious to find out about Andrea. So he gave her another phone number to contact him. Before Lily, Andrea had gone on trips with Calvin overseas. They went to Dubai and Mauritius, and she texted me every day while she was there. He bought her a nice handbag and some jewelry. He ‘spoiled her,’ as she would say. Lily also saw Dre and Calvin going into a hotel this past summer and called Calvin to talk to him about it. They broke up for a bit and then got back together. He would contact Andrea every now and again, but not as often as he did when he and Lily were broken up,” Emily finished.

“So Lily could be a suspect too. She could’ve found out that Calvin was still seeing your sister and wanted revenge,” Detective Williams said.

“Yeah,” Emily responded, wiping her nose with her sleeve again.

“Now tell us about Albert Little,” Detective Stevenson said.

“After Lily and Calvin got back together, he eventually proposed to her. Andrea saw a ring on Lily Bostitch’s page and a picture of her and Calvin. Things with Calvin slowed down a bit. Wait, let me back up a bit. It wasn't too long after meeting Calvin that Andrea got the new apartment and bought a new car. Between her on-again-off-again moments with Nicholas and her consistent escapades with Calvin, she was making enough money to afford a nice car and a place of her own. She moved out of the place she shared with Riley and Veronica. This was also around the time when I turned 17 and Child Protective Services was talking about moving me to another foster home. Andrea didn't like this idea, so she convinced me to apply for emancipation. I was still in Mama Kim's custody, so she said that she would support me in this decision. Andrea got the apartment in South Loop Chicago and the Mercedes. A little bit after that, I started going to Harold Washington Community College since it was downtown as well. Andrea not only wanted me to have a safe place to call home and not be in foster care anymore, but she also wanted me to keep an eye on the apartment while she would be away with her sugar daddies," Emily continued.

"So you mostly stayed home and went to classes?" Detective Williams asked.

"Yeah, and I did work study. I hung out with friends from time to time, but for the most part I stayed home and studied and kept in touch with Dre while she would be out galavanting with the three men. During this time, Nicholas was still sketchy, popping up every now and again. And things had slowed down with Calvin because of Lily finding out about them, and he was engaged then. This was around September or October. So that's when Dre realized that she needed a third sugar daddy to be able to pay for her car and place. That's when she connected with Albert Little. Albert Little is a surgeon, so he keeps long hours. He has a wife as well, Samantha Little; they've been married for 32 years and have three adult children. Albert is one of the top surgeons at the University of Illinois in Chicago hospital. He also teaches courses there. He and his wife recently separated, and that's when he decided to connect with a younger woman who he could spend his time with and money on. Out of all three of the men, Albert was the most possessive and clingy. He was erratic, and he hated when he found out that Dre had two other sugar daddies. He thought he was the only one. He told Dre that he really wanted to be with her and that she could drop Nicholas and Calvin because he would take care of her."

"And what did she say?" Detective Williams asked.

"She told him that she couldn't do that because she still had to take care of me. She didn't want anything serious, and she didn't sign up for this to be a full-time girlfriend. Albert disagreed and told her that's exactly what she was. They got into a fight about it, and Albert told her she'd better break up with Nicholas and Calvin, or else."

"What did he mean by or else?" Detective Stevenson asked.

"I don't know. When Andrea told me about it she said he looked upset and serious. She feared that he may cut her off and stop talking to her. She never felt like he would kill her. He still could have meant it that way," Emily said, looking down.

"You following all this?" Detective Williams asked Detective Stevenson.

"Yeah, definitely. So our suspects are Nicholas Wright because Andrea's dead body was found in the building his construction company is working on. His wife, because according to Emily, the wife didn't know about Andrea. Then Calvin Bruno — not really a suspect, but we should bring him in for questioning…"

"Calvin Bruno is a suspect. I forgot to mention that the last day I saw my sister, she was going to meet him," Emily interjected.

"Alright, that's some notable information. So Calvin Bruno is a suspect because Andrea was on her way to see him the last time Emily saw her. Lily Bostitch could be a suspect because of her anger about Calvin and Andrea's relationship. Then there is Albert Little because of his 'or else' comment to Andrea. Do you think Samantha Little is a suspect?"

"She might be; there is no telling what conversation she and Albert had about Andrea. We'll know once we talk to him," Detective Williams said.

"Then there is Andrea's phone and the daily text messages to Emily. Emily, can we see some of your text messages now?"

"Yeah sure." Emily pulled her phone out of her pocket and handed it over to the detectives.

"I'm going to scroll back to a week from now since Burgess said her body is over a week old. What did she say when you last saw her?" Detective Stevenson asked.

"She said she was going out to breakfast with Calvin before he headed to D.C. for a speaking engagement. He was on a discussion panel at a conference. Then she was supposed to have a dinner and movie date with Nicholas. She told me not to wait up for her, but I always tried to. So I saw her in the morning before she met Calvin, and I didn't see her again that day."

"So she met both of them the last day you saw her?" Detective Williams asked.

"She said she was going to. That was the last time I saw her. That was on Thursday, almost two weeks ago, on January 28th. Since then, it's been text messages."

"Today is February 9th, so Andrea could've died that night or the next day. Emily, when did you start having a feeling that Andrea wasn't telling you the truth about something in her text messages? Or in this case, maybe it wasn't her?" Detective Stevenson asked.

"It was February 1st. I had asked her why she had been gone for so long without calling me. If you look at the messages, you'll see that she told me that Calvin wanted her to come to D.C. with him, which was weird because Andrea didn't pack a suitcase. Then on February 4th, I asked her why she hadn't been home, and she told me that she got a call from Nicholas and that he wanted her to go to Florida with him. The weird part about it is, Andrea would always send me pictures or post pictures on social media when she went places. She didn't post or send me any pictures. The person texting me apologized for not sending pictures. Saying that D.C. was boring and there was nothing to post, and that she would show me the pictures from Florida when she got back. I felt that it was weird that she wasn't sending me any pictures, but I didn't think that my sister was…" Emily paused and put her head down again.

"Emily, you don't have to say anymore, you've given us more than enough information. And don't worry; with your help, we're going to find out who did this to Andrea," Detective Stevenson said.

"Can I call Mama Kim? I'm sure she's worried." Emily wiped her nose.

"Sure, I'll walk you to our phones while Detective Stevenson is looking through the text messages," Detective Williams stood up and escorted Emily to the phone to call Ms. Kimberly Baker. Once the two of them left the room, Detective Stevenson looked through Emily's phone and contacted the phone company for a copy of her phone records. She went back to the date of January 28th. The messages read:

> *Hey Em, I'm at breakfast with Calvin. He's going to be heading to D.C. soon. This place is nice, I gotta bring you here one day,* Andrea said at 8:15 am.

Okay, bring me back some of the food you're eating, Emily responded at 8:16 am.

Hey Em, Calvin asked me if I wanted to go to D.C. with him to the conference. I'm going to head to D.C. with him, but I really don't want to go. I think it's going to be kind of boring, Andrea said at 9:00 a.m.

Okay, just be careful. D.C. might be fun, Emily said at 9:05 a.m.

Yeah, but I don't want to sit at some conference all day, Andrea said at 9:07 a.m.

Don't worry, I'm sure it'll go by quickly, Emily said at 9:08 a.m.

The next conversation took place on January 29th.

Another day at the conference, Andrea said at 9:00 a.m.

How was it yesterday? Emily asked at 10:00 a.m.

Boring, like I thought it would be, but we went to a nice restaurant and he bought me a new outfit, Andrea said at 10:05 a.m.

Okay, that's fun, Emily said at 10:06 a.m.

Yeah, a friend of his has tickets to a game here so I guess we're going to a game tonight,

Andrea said at 10:08 a.m.

Have fun! Emily said at 10:09 a.m.

The next conversation took place on January 31st.

Hey Em, sorry for not texting yesterday. I'm on my way back home to Chicago. Calvin is done with the conference. It wasn't too bad I guess, Andrea said at 11:05 a.m.

I guess it wasn't. You didn't send any pictures, Emily said at 11:10 a.m.

I know, sorry about that. I'll be home soon and I'll show them to you when you come from class. There wasn't much to send besides the game, Andrea said at 11:12 a.m..

Hey, it's 5:00 and you're not home. Where are you? Emily said at 5:01 p.m..

The next conversation took place on February 1st.

Hey, why haven't you called me? You didn't come home last night. I haven't seen you in a few days. If you don't say anything I'm going to report you missing, Emily said at 10:00 a.m.

Sorry, I know I've been M.I.A. since going to the conference with Calvin. Nicholas texted me last night and I went to meet him, Andrea said at 10:15 a.m.

Okay, just let me know. I was worried when you didn't come home, Emily said at 10:17 a.m.

Don't worry, I'm just with Nicholas. I'll probably be home tomorrow, Andrea said at 10:20 a.m..

The next conversation took place on February 4th.

Dre where are you? I haven't seen you since the 28th, come home. Are you okay? It's getting lonely in this apartment, Emily said at 10:00 a.m.

Hey Em, I'm sorry, Nicholas surprised me with a trip to Florida last minute. I thought I told you, Andrea said at 10:15 a.m.

No you didn't. Is everything okay? Emily asked at 10:17 a.m.

Yeah Em, everything is fine. Don't worry, Andrea said at 10:20 a.m.

Okay, send me pictures of Florida or post them on Instagram. You didn't send or post any when you went to D.C. Emily said at 10:21 a.m..

Okay, I will! Andrea said at 10:23 a.m.

The next conversation took place on February 6th.

Hey Em, I'm still in Florida with Nicholas. We were in Miami now we're in Cape Coral, Andrea said at 12:00 p.m.

Okay, I have a test that I'm studying for. Why didn't you send me any pictures? Emily asked at 12:05 p.m.

I'll show them to you and post them as soon as I get home, Andrea said at 12:06 p.m.

When is that? Emily asked at 12:10 p.m.

Nicholas said we should be coming home in three days, Andrea said at 12:15 p.m.

Okay, great! I finally get to see you again. I've missed you, Emily said at 12:17 p.m.

The next conversation took place on February 9th, today.

Hey Em, we're on our way to the airport. We should be home in Chicago around noon, Andrea said at 8:00 a.m.

Okay, I'll see you then. We should get some brunch together, Emily said at 9:05 a.m.

Sounds good to me! Andrea said 9:07 a.m.

Hey, I'm on my way to Mama Kim's house. She says it's urgent. I hope everything is okay. If I'm not home when you come I'm still at her house, Emily said at 9:45 a.m.

After reading the messages, Detective Stevenson looked at her watch. She noticed that it was now 12:30 p.m. and there wasn't a response from the person. She thought Emily should send another text message soon and ask where Andrea was. Detective Stevenson became anxious and decided to step outside to show Detective Williams the messages. While Emily was still on the phone, Detective Williams was grabbing a cup of coffee.

"Hey, I looked at the messages. I went all the way back to January 28th. It shows that she was going to see Calvin Bruno. I think she could've died after her meeting with Calvin and before she supposedly met up with Nicholas."

"Okay, have they texted anything else today?" Detective Williams asked.

"No, and I'm worried."

"About what?"

"I think we shouldn't release Andrea Kane's name to the media."

"I don't think the chief will like that. He may have already contacted the media since Emily is here to confirm that the body we found was Andrea Kane."

"I know, but hear me out. If we found the person on the other end of the phone, we would find the killer. If the killer hears that the person found at the construction site was Andrea Kane, then they'd stop texting Emily. They'll realize that Emily knows Andrea is dead and we won't find out who has the phone. Then Nicholas Wright may try to flee because he and Andrea had a relationship. Her dead body was found at one of his construction sites, so he's the prime suspect — what's to keep him from fleeing?"

"Okay, Stevie, you got a point. I'll tell the chief the situation and that we should probably hold off releasing her name to the press."

"Tell him that he can give them a description of the body we found and how she was murdered, but not to give them a name. I'll have Officer Flores check to see the location that the last text was sent from," Detective Stevenson said to Detective Williams as he walked away with his coffee. Emily walked toward Detective Stevenson.

“Hey, Mama Kim didn’t take it too well. She’s really broken up about it. So what did you find when you looked at the messages?” Emily asked with her head down still wiping her nose with her sleeve.

“I’m sorry to hear that about Ms. Baker.”

“Once we find out who did this to my sister, Andrea will be at rest. That will help Mama Kim and me sleep better at night.”

“Well, I saw that the person who has your sister’s phone told you that they would be home by noon. It’s 12:35 p.m. now, why don’t you ask them where they are? See what they say.”

“Um…yeah, sure.” Emily grabbed her phone from Detective Stevenson. Her hands were shaking and they still had remnants of pizza crust and sauce on them. She didn’t care about any of that, but she worried about who might be on the other end of the phone. “What do I say?”

“Say whatever you would say if you knew that it was your sister,” Detective Stevenson said as Emily looked back down at the phone, hands still shaking as she texted.

Hey, you didn’t come home at 12:00. Is everything okay?

“Now what do I do?”

“Now you wait for them to respond.”

"What if they don't respond?" Her phone then vibrated and made a dinging noise to notify her that she just received a message. At that moment, Emily grew still, and chills trickled down her spines.

"Emily, is it from Andrea's phone?"

"Yeah, it says it's from her."

"Okay, read it."

Emily's hands shook even more. "It says,"

Sorry, I didn't come home at 12:00. We weren't on time for our flight, so we have to take the next flight out to Chicago.

"I can't believe they're still lying to me. Do they think I'm stupid?"

"No Emily, they know you aren't stupid. That's why they're coming up with so many different lies."

"Why are they doing this to me, as if they didn't already kill my sister? The one person I had in my life and they just took her away from me." Emily sat down.

"I know, and we will catch the person that did this. I told Williams to tell the chief that we're going to allow you to keep your phone and text this person. I'll have one of the officers check our system to see where the last message was sent from. We'll also hold off on announcing your sister's name on television."

"Why won't you announce her name on T.V.? I've already identified her body."

"Because if the person texting you finds out that you know about Andrea, they may not text back. And if Nicholas Wright finds out that it was Andrea who was dead in his building, he may try to flee."

"Okay," Emily looked down at the floor again.

"Do you want us to take you back to Ms. Baker's house to get your car?"

"No, um…that's not my car, that was Dre's car. I can just leave it at Mama Kim's house."

"Well we can take you home."

"I really don't want to go home either. I mean, knowing that Dre is dead, it's going to be hard staying there. I may end up doing something I may regret later."

"Well, where else can you go? Maybe a hotel? Do you have any money?"

"Can I stay here at the station? Can't you just put me in a cell for tonight?" Detective Stevenson stared at Emily, and as tears welled in

Emily's eyes, Detective Stevenson found herself getting misty-eyed too.

"I can only do that if you've committed a crime, Emily."

"You do it for homeless people all the time, right? Pretend that I'm homeless. I'm just some homeless foster kid whose sister just died…" Emily started to cry again.

"Hey, hey, you know, um…I really don't think you should stay here. Why don't — why don't you come stay at my house? It's just me, and since you want to be a part of the investigation anyway, it shouldn't be a problem." Detective Stevenson regretted every word and wondered what this might do for her position.

"Can you…can you do that?"

"Yeah, yeah, I can." Detective Stevenson knew she shouldn't have invited Emily to stay with her, but she pitied the poor foster kid with the drug addicted mother.

"Yeah, that works. I'll stay with you." Emily hugged Detective Stevenson. Even though she didn't know her, Emily knew she would be safe staying with the detective working on her sister's murder case. She sensed a position of authority, protection, and calm from

Detective Stevenson. Emily felt vulnerable and helpless now that Andrea was dead. “Thank you!”

“No problem, um…Emily, I have another question for you. Did any of your sister’s sugar daddies know where she lived or that you lived with her?”

“I don’t think they knew where Andrea lived. She wanted to keep me safe, so she never invited them over. She just met them out and stayed at hotels with them. That was one of her stipulations. She did tell them that I lived with her. Why do you ask?”

“Because I think it would be good for you to stay with me anyway. If one of her sugar daddies did this to her, who’s to say they won’t try to do something to you too? So I need to keep you safe, and you wouldn’t be safer anywhere else than with me.”

Detective Williams walked up to Emily and Detective Stevenson “Hey, so the chief is fine with us not releasing Andrea’s name to the public if it will interfere with our investigation. He’s also fine with Emily keeping her phone as long as we have the app and chip on it. I’d say today is your lucky day, Stevie.”

“That’s great. Emily got a text back from whoever has Andrea’s phone,” Detective Stevenson said.

"What did they say?" Detective Williams asked.

"They lied and said the flight was delayed," Emily angrily responded.

"That's horrible. How did Ms. Baker take it?" Detective Williams asked.

"Mama Kim took it the same way I did. I still can't believe Dre is gone."

"Well, it's almost 1:00. I put in for a warrant to arrest Mr. Wright, Mrs. Wright, and Calvin Bruno. Until tomorrow, there isn't much we can do." Detective Williams started to put his arms through his coat. "So I'm going to head home with my wife and children. I'm sure they'll be happy to see me. Stevenson, you need me for anything?"

"No, um…I'm just going to stay here with Emily. She's probably going to stop at Ms. Baker's house and pick up her car," Detective Stevenson lied to Detective Williams, immediately regretting it.

"Alright, I'll see you tonight for chili," Detective Williams walked out of the police station.

"Can we go to the site where you found my sister?" Emily asked once Detective Williams walked out.

"Yeah, I can take you there. It's still a crime scene, so we can go in. But are you sure you want to go?"

"Yeah, I want to go. I want to see where you all found my sister."

"Alright, let's go." Detective Stevenson walked out of the police station and drove Emily to the construction site where they found Andrea dead. During the car ride neither of them said anything until Emily had a few questions.

"So you don't have a husband and kids?"

"No, I just pour myself into work so I haven't had the time," Detective Stevenson responded.

"Oh. You know you remind me of her."

"Of who?"

"My sister. She was caring, like you. She poured herself into her work, but she was focused on taking care of the people she cared about. I'm glad that you're the detective for her case," Emily said looking out of the window and not making eye contact with the detective.

"Well I'll take that as a compliment. Thank you. Your sister sounds like she was a wonderful person." Detective Stevenson smiled.

“She was. When we were little and our mom would leave us home for days, I was always scared. I would cry, and it would be hard for me to go to sleep. Andrea would sing to me and make me Spaghetti O’s in the microwave. They were disgusting, but that’s all we had to eat. Even though she would tell me not to worry, I could tell she was scared too. She would never tell me she was scared, but I knew she was. She was always focused on protecting me,” Emily said.

“I always wished I had a big sister. Someone to look out for me like Andrea looked out for you.”

“Having a big sister was the best thing I ever had. Even though you didn’t have one, you seem like you would be a good one,” Emily said as she and Detective Stevenson pulled up to the construction site.

“Thanks, Emily. We’re here.”

Detective Stevenson parked the car. As she and Emily exited, Emily just stood there staring at the construction site that once housed her sister’s dead body. She walked up to Detective Stevenson where she held up the yellow tape so Emily could enter the site. They walked through the gravel, stepped on the concrete, and entered the partially finished building. Detective Stevenson walked over to the spot where Andrea previously lay dead.

“This is where the construction workers found her. She was buried under the bags of concrete mix.”

“I see what you mean by there not being any blood. I only see a little blood in this spot where they found her.” Emily bent down to look at the spot where Andrea was. “Do you think they killed her here?”

“No, we believe she was transported. Maybe in a trash bag. She was also frozen, which is why there wasn’t any blood. And since she was at a construction site, where there are no windows, doors, walls, or heat, her body stayed frozen.”

“Detective Stevenson?”

“Yes Emily?”

“Can we go to your place now? I just need some rest.”

“Yes Emily, we can go to my place.”

“And can you promise me that whoever did this to my sister, you’ll make sure that they rot in jail?” Emily started crying again as she bent down by the spot where her sister’s dead body had lain.

“I’ll make sure of it.”

“Good, because rotting in hell wouldn’t be enough for what they did to my sister. I want them to suffer in this life and the next.”

Part 2: The Detectives

Chapter 3 - Detectives Stevenson & Williams

After revisiting the crime scene, Detective Stevenson finally took Emily Kane back to her one-bedroom, open-concept condo in downtown Chicago. Once they entered, Emily walked in and looked around in disbelief at how small and unkept it was. She noticed that there wasn't much furniture or belongings in Detective Stevenson's home. There were papers everywhere and clothes on the floor in her room, even though there was a washer and dryer inside her condo. She had dirty dishes in the sink, her bed wasn't made, and there were no pets, no decorations, and no television, just a radio in the corner of her living room. There was one couch and no chairs. Everything looked like it came from either a second hand store or was passed on to her. Either way, Emily wasn't impressed with Detective Stevenson's place. She'd expected more; she'd expected it to be a lot nicer, cleaner, and nicely decorated with furniture that matched.

"Here's my place. It's really small, but there should be enough room for us both. You can sleep in the bedroom, and I'll sleep on the couch. Or you can sleep on the couch if you're not comfortable sleeping in my room. There is a bathroom through here, and the kitchen and living room are combined, as you can see. You're free to eat whatever you want." Detective Stevenson opened the cabinets and fridge where there were a few cans, condiments, and take-out containers. "I know you don't have any of your belongings yet, but you know, whenever you're ready to go get them, we can," Detective Stevenson said.

"Are you a minimalist?" Emily asked.

"Um…I don't know what you mean," Detective Stevenson responded, staring at Emily.

Emily didn't want to come across as judgemental. She was the girl that had grown up in a home with a mother who was on drugs, so her living conditions had been less than adequate. When she'd left her mother's custody and moved in with her grandmother and Mama Kim, they'd had comfortable homes filled with decorations, furniture, odds and ends that held a story, home-cooked meals, and smells of food cooking. Detective Stevenson's home felt more like the home where she'd lived with her biological mother. Regardless, she was appreciative that Detective Stevenson allowed her to stay with her until she felt ready to go back home, or with Mama Kim, or wherever.

"I just mean you don't like a lot of furniture, or stuff, or clutter?" Emily asked.

"Oh, well I guess. I'm usually not here. I'm always working."

"You don't ever have people over?"

"No, my family lives in Alabama, I'm the only one here."

"No friends?"

"Not many, my work keeps me busy. I have work friends and family, and when they have get-togethers at their house, I usually go over. That reminds me — Williams' wife, Cheryl, is cooking chili tonight. I told him I would come by. I can just tell him I don't have to..."

"No, you can go, I'll be okay," Emily interrupted.

"Well, I don't want to just leave you here by yourself. If that was going to be the case you could've gone home."

"I know, but I don't want you to miss your plans. And if I wasn't invited, I shouldn't show."

"No, Williams and Cheryl won't mind. I wouldn't be surprised if they'll have more people over. You should come. I think it'll be good to take your mind off of everything for a while."

"Maybe." Even though Emily was unsure about going, she was glad that they could actually go somewhere and have a home-cooked meal. She assumed that Detective Stevenson didn't cook. "Do you go over their house for dinner a lot?"

"Sometimes, I don't really cook much," Detective Stevenson said as Emily nodded because she realized she was right. "Well, we have some time before we go over there, and we can't start making arrests until tomorrow, so is there something you want to do?"

"Well, I'm not hungry or anything. I just want to find out who killed my sister." Emily looked down at her sweater and finally saw all of the dried-up mucus on her sleeves.

"Do you want to rest? I mean, you've had a rough morning." Detective Stevenson watched Emily walk through her tiny condo, looking at everything.

"No, I'm fine." Emily sat down on the couch.

"Okay then, I guess I'll get some work done," Detective Stevenson sat down to work on the papers that were set on her small table by her kitchen.

"Are any of those papers for my sister's case?"

"Oh, no, this is some more paperwork I need to get done. I was going to start writing things about your sister's case on sticky notes and sticking them to my wall. It's like creating a puzzle and piecing everything together."

"How did you become a detective? Sorry if I'm asking too many questions…"

"No, it's fine. That's why you're so smart, you ask a lot of questions. Well, the story of how I became a detective is a long one."

"We have nothing but time. You can tell me how you ended up in Chicago, how you moved here from Alabama, why you don't cook, and why you have so little furniture."

"Are we still on that? I thought I explained that to you." Detective Stevenson smiled as she glanced at Emily. "Well, I guess I just followed in my family's footsteps. My father was a cop in Alabama. Never became a detective because he wanted to spend as much time with us, his family, as possible. He was offered the promotion to become a detective, but he didn't take it because he knew it would take him away from his family. My dad's father was a detective. He didn't get to spend a lot of time with his children, but he became the first Black detective in our county in Alabama. So, I wanted to be like my father and my grandfather. I was a cop for six years and then I was offered the promotion to become a detective."

"How do you and your family feel, being Black cops?"

"I can say it's a very polarizing identity. I mean, as you know since you asked the question, Black people haven't had the best experience with law enforcement. I think my grandfather was trying to change that, and he wanted to become a cop to show children in our community that you can be Black and wear blue. A lot of children looked up to my grandfather when he became a cop, including my dad. But he endured many trials from the police department, his brothers in blue, and his brothas in the neighborhood. He had to find his way — he wasn't completely accepted by the department and some of the Black people in his neighborhood didn't approve. Things got a lot better once my father's generation came along. My father still endured some hatred, but he learned from his father's mistakes how to handle things. He was loved more by the people in his neighborhood and everyone knew that they could count on him. By the time my father became a cop, there were more Black cops, so he had a brothahood of brothas in blue. My grandfather became a detective after 10 years of service as a police officer, which is much longer than it usually takes. He was determined to honor this position and live up to it. He wanted to make sure he did everything perfectly so he could open the door for other Black detectives."

"That's awesome!"

"Yeah, but it didn't always feel like that. There were some cases that never got the attention they needed and that made my grandfather feel as if he wasn't making a difference."

"What do you mean?" Emily sat on the couch and turned towards Detective Stevenson as she organized her papers.

"Well, when my grandfather first became a detective, a young girl in our neighborhood was found dead in an abandoned building."

"Like my sister?"

"Yes, but this young lady was Black, and unlike the care and attention that your sister's case will get, this young lady's case didn't get any attention at all. It was a murder mystery that went unsolved. A cold case, as they call it." Detective Stevenson held her head down in sadness.

"I'm sorry," Emily said, dropping her eyes to the ground and looking down at her hands. "That's not fair."

"It's not fair, and it's not your fault. The issues that Blacks and Whites have with one another were here long before you and I. Anyway, instead of continuing to ask the department to focus on this case, my grandfather decided to find out for himself. He started asking questions from people in the neighborhood, getting the scoop, and he eventually found out who killed this young lady. He was able to give her parents peace of mind. They were always nice people in the neighborhood. My grandfather had known them growing up, so he didn't want to let them down. He was able to arrest the man who murdered her, and he put him behind bars for the rest of his life."

"He sounds like a superhero."

"He was, a bit. He was my superhero." Detective Stevenson smiled.

"He and your father must have been proud of you when you decided to become a cop."

"Ha, not at all," Detective Stevenson laughed. "I didn't get any support from my father and grandfather. I grew up with two brothers, and my grandfather and father expected them to become cops too."

"Did they?"

"Not at all. My eldest brother became a chef, and my other brother became a pilot. My eldest brother still lives in Alabama, but my other brother stays in California. I'm an aunt — each of them has a wife and two children."

"So they didn't want you to become a cop because you're a girl?"

"Yeah, exactly. My grandfather and father thought, *What place does a girl have in the police department?* I understand they were worried about my well-being, especially with me being a Black woman in a predominantly White-male profession. They didn't want me going through what they had gone through, or worse. But I knew how to handle myself. I'd learned from the best. Anyway, when I decided to become a police officer, I was in Alabama. I only worked there one year. It was great, but I felt like I wanted more action, and I wanted to leave home. Not having my family's support made being a cop in Alabama more complicated. I saw all of the chaos that was happening in Chicago and decided to transfer here. They needed more cops, I knew this was the action that I wanted, and I got the support that I was always looking for when I came here. The police department here was happy that someone wanted to be a part of the craziness in Chicago. I worked as an officer in Chicago for five years and then became a detective. I've been a detective for five years now. I had many partners for the past three years, but then in my fourth year, Williams became my partner. He's been the best partner I could ask for. He's super supportive, and we can bounce ideas off of each other. He's more like a brother than my actual brothers. I haven't really talked to my family for a couple of years now."

"Do you ever feel lonely? I mean you said your brothers have wives and children, but you're not around family, you live here alone, and you throw yourself into work."

"You're right, you do ask a lot of questions," Detective Stevenson laughed.

"No, I was just wondering. You don't have children, or a spouse. You said you throw yourself into work. You don't take pride in where you live. You don't spend much time at home. All because you feel lonely, right?"

"So you think you have me all figured out?"

"Well, I am a psychology major," Emily said, smiling.

"Well that explains it." Detective Stevenson smiled. "You'd make a great detective with all that psychoanalyzing."

"Thanks." Emily blushed.

"Well, there may be some truth to what you're saying. I always wanted to be a detective like my grandfather, and I knew that I couldn't do that if I had a family like my father. I guess I just never focused on making a family because I didn't want them to get in the way of my dream of becoming a detective. I never go back home to Alabama because it's too chaotic. I don't visit my brother in California because he's always busy. So, work is just all I have."

"That sucks."

"Okay psychology major, what do you suggest I do?" Detective Stevenson joked as she put her papers away.

"Well, I think you should put yourself out there more. You know, do something besides work and helping some random foster kid whose sister was just murdered. Have fun and enjoy yourself a bit more. And try forgiving your dad and grandad and go home. My mom did some harsh things — she was so bad at being a mom that I didn't even care about getting her support for anything. She was neglectful, self-centered, uncaring, and unloving. I wish all I needed from her was her support."

"Your teachers were right, you are smart." Detective Stevenson smiled.

"Thanks." Emily smiled with pride.

"So why did you choose to go into psychology?"

"Part of the reason was because it seemed interesting. Like you said, psychoanalyzing people seemed cool. But deep down, the real reason was because I wanted to understand my mom and my sister more. I wanted to understand why they were so irrational and made such poor decisions. I couldn't understand how my mother could be raised by my grandmother, who was amazing, and become such a horrible mother herself. Or how she ended up on drugs and treated me and Dre the way she did. Then I wanted to understand how Dre could be raised by someone like that and then turn around and do something so reckless." Emily looked down at her hands sadly. "Thank you for allowing me to come and stay with you. It has helped to take my mind off of everything."

"Of course, I'm glad I could. Do you know where your mom might be?"

"I think I know where she is," Emily said, looking at the wall ahead of her.

"You do? You don't think you should tell her about Andrea?"

"Why would she care? She didn't care about us when we were kids, and she doesn't care about us now. I don't think she cares if we live or die," Emily responded in anger.

"I still think she deserves to know. She's your mom, and she was Andrea's mom. She brought you both into this world, she would want to know if you weren't okay."

"I don't know."

"If you want to go, I'll take you. I'll be there to protect you and support you."

"Can you arrest her? Because I'm sure she'll be high."

“No, Emily. Unless she’s selling drugs I can’t just arrest her for getting high.”

“Well, I guess we can go.” Emily hopped up off the couch and walked towards the door.

“You mean now?” Detective Stevenson glanced over to the door where Emily was standing.

“Yeah, let’s go before I change my mind,” Emily said, opening the door.

“So where is your mom?” Detective Stevenson asked as they entered the elevator of her condo building.

“She’s in a trap house in the Austin neighborhood. That’s where she’s been for the past couple of years. Andrea would stop by and visit her and give her money. I told her to stop doing that, and that she was only supporting her habit. All she was going to do was buy drugs with the money.”

“I know, but I’m sure Andrea just wanted to take care of your mom like she was trying to take care of you.”

“I know. She tried to get her to go to rehab, but she never wanted to.”

"Emily, I know your mom has hurt you all, but she's sick. She's so sick she doesn't know how to be a good mother."

"No, she's not sick. She's on drugs." Emily looked up at Detective Stevenson before getting off the elevator on the main floor.

Detective Stevenson and Emily entered the car after exiting her building. They drove thirty minutes from Detective Stevenson's condo in West Loop to the trap house in Austin. As they rode from West Loop to Austin, they both couldn't help but notice and comment on the rapid change in neighborhood appearance. What was once a neighborhood surrounded by stores, restaurants, high-rise condo buildings, people shopping and walking their dogs, grocery stores, and clean streets in West Loop had slowly changed to a food desert of a neighborhood that had boarded up buildings, vacant lots, two flats and apartment buildings, guys standing outside selling drugs, food chain restaurants, littered streets, and corner markets.

"Good ol' Chicago, gotta love the rapid change in neighborhood appearance. Just shows the difference in income, I guess. Those with higher incomes get better neighborhoods," Detective Stevenson said bitterly.

"This is the house here," Emily said as Detective Stevenson stopped on a block with many vacant lots, abandoned buildings, and boarded up houses. There were men and women walking up and down the street, stumbling over every step as they were walking, talking to themselves, and fighting with their demons. Emily was about to step out of the car and walk up to the trap house where her mom had been staying to knock on the door. A man and woman, too high to be considered conscious, sat on the porch, as though they were asleep. Emily sat in the car for a moment processing how she would break the news to her mother. She jumped out of the car, and noticing her fear, Detective Stevenson jumped out of the car behind her to walk up to the trap house.

"Wait Emily, I'll go knock on the door."

"Why, you're the police, they're not going to open it for you," Emily said.

"Oh yes they will," Detective Stevenson banged on the door. "This is Detective Stevenson, open up." After she knocked on the door, a young man opened the door, looking confused.

"Yeah, Detective?" the young man said as Detective Stevenson showed her badge.

“I’m not here for any trouble. This young lady just wants to see her mother.”

“Oh, that’s one of Alexis’s daughters. Come in,” the young man responded.

“No, I want you to go get her. Tell her to come out here,” Detective Stevenson said authoritatively.

“Aight, here she come,” the young man walked back into the house.

“Don’t expect her to be fully comprehensible,” Emily looked down on the ground and folded her arms.

“I wasn’t.” Detective Stevenson turned around to Emily. Afterwards, Emily’s mom walked out. It was bitter cold outside, but she was only wearing a tank top and pajama pants. She looked confused and scared.

“Are you here to arrest me, Detective?” Alexis asked. “I didn’t do anything wrong.”

“No, I’m just escorting your daughter, Emily, here. She has something very important to tell you.”

“Did she get arrested? If so, she ain’t in my custody no more,” Alexis said frantically, shaking.

"No ma'am, I'm not here to arrest anybody, and no one has been arrested. She just has something she needs to tell you."

"Hey baby, how you doin? You look good," Alexis said, but Emily didn't respond. "Where is your sister? Where is my Dre? I haven't seen her in a while. She usually comes to bring me money." Emily just stood there, slowly shedding her tears as she looked up at her mother. Emily hadn't seen her mother since they were put in their grandmother's custody. Emily couldn't help but notice her mother's appearance. She looked so frail, dirty, and disheveled. She kept holding her arms because she was cold, wiping her nose as mucus ran down, and her arms had so many sores on them because she had used so many needles to get high. *Why did this have to be her mother?* Emily thought. *Why did Andrea leave her to tell their mother about her death?*

"Emily, baby, what's wrong?"

"Andrea is dead," Emily bluntly stated as she just stood there with her head down, still crying.

"What?" Alexis paused for a moment staring at Emily. Noticing Emily still crying she responded, "No, no, that's not true. You're lying, why are you lying to me?" Alexis asked frantically as Emily still stood there crying.

"I'm afraid that it is true, ma'am. Andrea was found lying dead at a construction site yesterday. Emily came by to identify the body today."

"No, no, it's not true. My baby ain't dead, that wasn't her." Alexis started crying.

"Ma'am, that was…"

"Get away from here, just leave me alone. Emily, don't lie to me like that. Don't come back here. Tell Andrea she can come back, not you." Alexis stepped back in the house. Emily just jumped back in the car, waiting for Detective Stevenson to come back in. She slammed the door and sat crying. Detective Stevenson came down the stairs, got in the car on the driver's side, and looked at Emily.

"Emily, you…"

"Can we just go back to your house?" Emily sat in the passenger seat, crying, her hair covering most of her face.

"Yeah, sure." Detective Stevenson put the key in the ignition and started driving off. "I was just going to tell you that you did the right thing by telling your mom about your sister."

“It doesn’t feel like it.”

“Sometimes doing the right thing doesn’t feel good, but it’s still right no matter how it feels.” The thirty-minute drive back to her condo was long and quiet.

They were finally back at Detective Stevenson’s condo when Emily asked,

“Do you have something I can wear? I need to shower, and I don’t want to look like this when we go over Detective Williams’ house for chili.”

“Yeah, I’ll get you something, and some towels.” Emily stood wiping her eyes with her sleeve. “I’ll give you a sweater and some jeans, since it’s cold out.”

“That’s fine.” Detective Stevenson handed her some clothes and towels.

“This is what’s clean. I haven’t done my laundry in a couple of days.”

“No worries, thanks.” Emily walked into the bathroom, turned on the shower, stripped down, entered the shower, let the water hit her head, and wept. She wept in the same manner that she wept when she first found out about Andrea’s death. She wept because her sister was dead. She wept because she was scared to go home. She wept because she didn't want to see Mama Kim because she'd be sad too. She wept because of her mom. She wept because her grandma was dead. And she wept because she felt so alone. At 18, she was all alone, without her mother, her grandmother, and her sister, no father, no place to stay, nothing. After 20 minutes of crying and standing under the water, she turned off the shower, dried off, put on the clothes that Detective Stevenson gave her, and she was ready to head to Detective Williams house for chili. She couldn't wait to be in a different environment to take her mind off of everything again.

She walked out of the bathroom, hair still wet, nails bitten, faced wiped of tears, and said,

"I'm ready."

"Okay, good. I just texted Williams — he said we can come over now."

"Did he say *we* could come over?"

"Not exactly, I was going to let him know the situation once I got there. Williams is cool, he'll understand. Let's go."

Detective Stevenson and Emily drove up to Detective Williams' home on the south side of Chicago. Emily was in awe at how beautiful his home was. Even though Emily was happy not to be home at this moment, she was nervous about entering someone's house that she didn't know to eat dinner. Not to mention, it was the detective for his sister's case. She felt comfortable knowing that Detective Stevenson would be there to defend her coming. Both of them walked up to the door and Detective Stevenson knocked on it. Emily just stood with her arms folded and her head down.

"Don't be nervous, it'll be fine. I'll explain everything to Williams." Detective Williams answered the door.

"Hey Stevie," Detective Williams said. He stood for a minute, shocked to see Emily standing with Detective Stevenson. "Hey Emily?" he said, wondering what she was doing there.

"I'll explain in a sec," Detective Stevenson said.

"Stevenson." Detective Williams shook his head and sighed. "Come in, you two." Emily waved hello as she walked in with Detective Stevenson.

"Hey Stevie," Cheryl, Detective Williams' wife, said as she walked up to hug Detective Stevenson. "How have you been?"

“I’m great, Cheryl, thanks for allowing me to come to dinner tonight.”

“Of course, you know you’re family to us. Who is this?” Cheryl asked, pointing to Emily.

“This is a friend of mine, Emily Kane.” Detective Stevenson beckoned Emily to come forward. Emily came forward to shake Cheryl’s hand.

“Hi, you have a beautiful home,” Emily said somewhat quietly, holding her hand out.

“Hi Emily! Give me a hug, we love to hug in this house.” Cheryl went in to hug Emily. Emily wasn’t used to hugging people, especially people she didn’t know. But at this moment, it was nice to have a hug. She didn’t realize how much she needed it. Since finding out about her sister’s death, no one had given her a hug like that. “Would you like to help me with the toppings for the chili?”

“Yeah, sure.” Emily walked away with Cheryl, talking to her about the chili.

“Stevenson,” Detective Williams said, beckoning Detective Stevenson to come into his office, “Come here, I need to talk to you about our…case.” Detective Stevenson knew Detective Williams wanted to ask her what she was doing with Emily. Detective Williams closed the door and stood looking at Detective Stevenson, waiting for her to respond.

“She needed a place to stay,” Detective Stevenson responded as Detective Williams hung his head.

“She has a place to stay, Stevenson, her sister’s apartment, a hotel, or even with Ms. Baker.”

“I know, but she really didn’t want to go home today. She had a rough morning. She lost the one person she truly had in her life. She found out her sister was dead today. She had to tell her foster mother, and she can’t go back and stay with her, she has two children there already. She also had to tell her biological mother today…”

“Wait, you found her biological mother?”

“Emily knew where she was, and I convinced her to tell her mom.”

“How did her mom take it? Where was she?”

“She was in a trap house in the Austin neighborhood. She was stoned, Williams, she looked so bad. When Emily told her that Andrea was dead, she didn’t believe her.”

“How often does she go to see her biological mother?”

"Emily doesn't go to see her, Andrea would. She would go by to see her and give her money."

"To buy more drugs?"

"Basically, yeah."

"Do you think she could be a suspect?"

"I don't know, we could always check into it. But I have a hard time believing she would've killed Andrea and put her body at one of her sugar daddies' buildings."

"You got a point. Well if anything leads us to her, we know where to find her. I'm sure she ain't going anywhere anytime soon. So how long is Emily going to stay with you?"

"I don't know. I just planned for this day, but I don't know. This girl has been through so much in her life. This is just another blow to her. I didn't want to be another person to let her down and put her in a hotel somewhere. I'm worried about her."

"Do you think she may harm herself?"

"I don't know, and I don't want to take that chance to find out."

"When was the last time Emily texted her sister's phone?"

"When we were at the police station."

"Well it's almost five now, why don't you tell her to send another one. We'll bring Nicholas Wright and his wife in tomorrow for questioning. Then the chief will announce that the body we found was Andrea Kane's to the media later on tomorrow night."

"That soon?"

"Yeah, the chief doesn't want to wait any longer. So you and Emily better come up with a plan as to how you're going to respond to the person on the other end of her sister's phone."

"Okay, can we eat some chili now? I'm really hungry," Detective Stevenson tried to change the conversation.

"Go ahead, Stevie," Detective Williams opened the door to his office and they both walked out.

"What were you two talking about?" Cheryl asked as both detectives came back to the kitchen.

"Oh, you know, work stuff," Detective Williams said.

"Always," Cheryl said. "Emily has been great at helping me get everything prepared."

"Thank you," Emily said quietly, smiling.

"Michael, can you go get the kids so we can start eating?" Cheryl asked Detective Williams.

"I'm on it." Detective Williams walked upstairs to grab the boys.

"How many children do you have?" Emily asked.

"We have six year old twin boys. Get ready, Emily, they're wild and rambunctious," Cheryl said. "So Emily, are you Detective Stevenson's mentee or intern?" Cheryl asked, but Emily didn't know how to respond. She looked at Detective Stevenson to answer for her.

"Yeah, she's my mentee. She attends Harold Washington Community College and is studying psychology, but she has shown an interest in being a Detective. I went to her school to speak one day, and she asked if she could be my mentee," Detective Stevenson lied to Cheryl. Emily just looked at her. She didn't know Detective Stevenson could lie so well.

"That's awesome," Cheryl said, smiling.

"WHOA! Here are our boys." Detective Williams brought the boys downstairs out of their room. They had their arms and legs crossed around their father's legs. "Crazy as can be. Go take a seat, you two, so we can eat."

"Baby, are you mentoring Emily too?" Cheryl asked.

"What?" Detective Williams looked confused as he sat down with the boys at the table. Detective Stevenson just gave him a look to tell him to go along with the lie.

"Oh. No, just Stevie."

"Well, Emily, you're in good hands. These are two of the finest detectives in Chicago. And an added bonus is that they're both Black. I mean, how many Black female and male Black detective duos do you know?" Cheryl asked as she set the chili and all of its toppings on the table.

"Not very many, and I can tell that they're both great detectives already," Emily said as they all sat down to eat, not making eye contact. "Thank you both for welcoming me into your home, it's really nice, and I really appreciate it. And this chili looks amazing."

"It's our pleasure, Emily." Detective Williams grabbed the cornbread and passed it to Emily.

"Auntie Stevie, sit next to me," one of Detective Williams' kids said.

"Alright, nephew," Detective Stevenson responded.

"So… um, Detective Stevenson told me about her life in Alabama and how she became a detective here in Chicago. Can you tell me how you became a detective and how you met your wife, Detective Williams?" Emily asked. Detective Williams looked a bit confused at Emily and glanced over at Detective Stevenson, who was confused as well.

"Oh Emily, you don't want to know that." Detective Williams eating his chili.

"No, I do. I'm kind of interested in this whole detective thing," Emily went along with the lie Detective Stevenson told Cheryl.

"Well, I grew up here in Chicago. I grew up on the west side of Chicago, a very rough and chaotic neighborhood. But I stayed focused on my studies to make my way out. Um…being a Black man in Chicago, the cops weren't always a role model. There is a long, horrible, deadly relationship between Black men and cops. But one day, a Black cop was assigned to our neighborhood. He was cool and strong, authoritative but down to earth, you know. He was one of us, he protected us, and he cared for us. I saw him and wanted to be him. My mother always wanted me to go to college. I'm currently in a doctoral program working on my Ph.D. as well, but when I told my mother about becoming a cop, she wasn't thrilled. She didn't understand what I was trying to do, but I told her that I was trying to become the change I wanted to see in the world. She understood this; she didn't agree with it, but she supported me either way. I worked for five years as a police officer with the CPD and became a detective. This is my third year as detective and my second year with Stevie, my big sister in the field. I wanted to be a detective because I felt that there were a lot of unsolved cases about Black people that I wanted to help to solve. Not only do our lives matter, but bringing peace to the ones we love once we're gone matters too. That's why I'm a detective."

"That's great. How does your mom feel about everything now?" Emily asked.

"Well she's proud to say that her Black son is a detective and will soon have a Ph.D. She's more than proud." Detective Williams said proudly.

"You forgot to tell her how you met me, baby," Cheryl said.

"I didn't forget, I was saving the best part for last," Detective Williams responded as everyone at the table laughed. "My wife, Dr. Williams, has a doctorate in education. She was a teacher in my old neighborhood, at my old neighborhood school. I was assigned to be one of the cops at the school. Me and some other guys on the force would sit outside when the kids arrived at school and play basketball with them, and we came back when the kids dismissed from school. We wanted to show them that they were safe with us, that we cared for them, and that we were watching out for them. There were and still are a lot of shootings in my old neighborhood, so we were there to protect the kids on their way to and from school. While I was working I saw a very beautiful teacher. She taught third grade. She would arrive early and leave late. I would walk her to her car when she left late, and I would carry her things into the building for her in the morning."

Cheryl blushed and smiled. "I thought he laid it on pretty thick, but he was cute."

"She was this beautiful Nubian goddess who the kids seemed to love, and she loved them. When I would walk her to her car, she talked to me about how much she loved being a teacher. She was working towards becoming a principal. At the time, she was working on getting her license. She was from the neighborhood, like me, and was focused on making it better, one step at a time. One day, I asked her out. She told me that she didn't want to date a cop, even if he was Black. I told her that when I took her out, I would take off the uniform. She asked me what I meant by that. I told her I meant whatever she wanted me to mean. After many failed attempts, the next school year, she allowed me to take her out. We got married a year later. Then three years later, we had thing one and thing two over here. We've been in love since our first date. Did I tell the story right, baby?" Detective Williams asked as he kissed his wife on the cheek.

"Yes, you did. But I wasn't in love with you after our first date. It was more after the third date," Cheryl said as everyone laughed. Even Emily laughed, the first time she'd done so all day.

"Thank you for telling me that, it was very nice," Emily said.

"Of course, thank you for listening," Detective Williams responded.

"Detective Stevenson told me that it's hard to be a detective and have a family. Is it like that for the two of you?" Emily asked.

"I do keep long hours, and Cheryl's job as a principal isn't easy either, but we have a lot of help with our children. Cheryl has her mother, father, and sister who help out with the kids. I have my mother who help us with the kids. So we have our village that helps us raise them," Detective Williams responded.

"Yes, my job isn't as hard as Michael's job, but being a principal can be difficult as well because I have to work long hours sometimes too, and I miss him when he's gone for work so much. But like he said, we have a village and the chief and Stevie are very understandable about Michael needing to be home with his family," Cheryl responded. "If you want to make it work, it definitely can."

"Well I'm sure you can see Emily Williams and Cheryl are perfect," Detective Stevenson responded as everyone laughed.

The rest of the night went well. Everyone ate their chili and cornbread and the detectives shared more stories about their jobs and different cases they've solved together. Detective Williams put the boys to sleep, and Cheryl walked Emily and Detective Stevenson out. As they headed back to Detective Stevenson's condo, they realized that tomorrow was the day that they would arrest the Wrights for Andrea's case.

"You seemed like you enjoyed yourself," Detective Stevenson said, gladly smiling at Emily's joy.

"I did, Cheryl was really nice. Thanks for encouraging me to go," Emily said.

"Of course, I knew it would take your mind off of everything. Are you ready for tomorrow?"

"Yeah, I want to find out who killed my sister. I won't rest until I find out." Emily stared out the passenger window.

"It's 7:00 now — you haven't texted your sister's number since 12:30 this afternoon. You should text them again."

"Yeah, I should." Emily took out her phone and sent a text to her sister's number.

"The chief wants to announce your sister's name to the media tomorrow night after we confront the Wrights and bring them in for questioning. You okay with that?"

"I am, but I don't think I really have a choice."

"Yeah. You can stay with me as long as you want, but what are you going to do about your sister's apartment and car?"

"Well, once they announce her death on T.V., I'm sure I'll have to move out anyway. I'll keep the car. I'll find somewhere else to go, I guess."

"I'm behind you, whatever you want to do."

"Are you behind me in becoming a detective, too? You lied pretty well and pretty quickly to Cheryl."

"Hey, I'm a detective. I hear people lie all day. And if you're really serious about it, I support that too. What did you text?"

"I just asked them if they're coming home tonight. I can't wait for them to announce it to the media so I can tell whoever this is that I know they're lying."

"I can't wait too." An alert came to Emily's phone — it was a text message from Andrea's number.

> *Hey, are you coming home tonight?* Emily said at 7:05 p.m.
>
> *Not tonight, I met back up with Calvin. I'll see you tomorrow morning,* the person texted at 7:09 p.m.

"They texted back, they said they're not coming back home. They're out with Calvin." Emily shook her head in disbelief at all the lies the person was telling. "Hey, the person hasn't mentioned Albert yet, do you think it could be him?"

"Could be, but we can't come up with a conclusion until we get the suspects' narratives. We have to check with their alibis as well. So this could take some time. Make sure you get some sleep tonight," Detective Stevenson said as they drove into the parking garage of her condo building and parked her car.

"I probably won't get any sleep tonight, but I'll still be ready for tomorrow," Emily said, unbuckling her seat belt.

Part 3 : The Suspects

Chapter 4 - Nicholas & Amber Wright

It was 6:00 a.m., February 10th, and Detective Stevenson and Emily were getting ready to head to the police station. This day was gloomier than the day before; it was raining, it was cold, the roads were icy, and there was a bit of snow on the ground from the night before. As Emily showered that morning, there were no tears in her eyes, only anger. There was no pain in her heart, only rage. Instead of having her head down and her arms folded, she held her head up and clenched her fists. She felt that deep down one of her sister's sugar daddies had killed her, and the fact that her sister was found in Nicholas Wright's building made him seem even more suspicious. When she was completely dressed, she opened the bathroom door. Detective Stevenson was already dressed, badge on and gun on her hip.

“Hey, you look better this morning,” Detective Stevenson said as Emily exited the bathroom.

“I’m just ready to find my sister’s killer.”

“I know, but I gotta warn you that it may not be that easy. Nicholas Wright and his wife could have an alibi. We may find out today that it’s not him or her. Even once we’re done questioning them and move towards the other suspects, we have to find evidence, or get a confession. Then there are trials. It could take years to find your sister’s murderer or years to convict them for murder. I just want to make you aware,” Detective Stevenson told Emily.

“I know, but starting this process is one step in the right direction.”

“Yes it is, and it’s because of you that we have all this information. The knowledge about your sister’s life that we needed to identify these suspects and make these connections — it’s all because of you. Are you sure you’re ready for this today?”

“Yes, I’m ready.”

"Okay. We'll have coffee and breakfast at the police station. Williams is going to pick some up for us on his way there. You'll be behind the window watching the interrogation with the chief. Williams and I will be in the interrogation room with Wright and his wife at separate times."

"Do you have to go to their house first? Or will they be at the police station already?"

"Williams and I will have to go to their home to take the wife in for questioning. If Wright is there we'll take him in for questioning too. If he's not there, we'll stop by his office as well to see if he's there. But you, young lady, will be at the police station while all of this is happening."

"Wait, why? I want to come too."

"Emily, while we're gathering suspects for questioning, you can't come with us. That part we can't allow. You're already staying with me, and you're a big part of this case because of your phone and the connection to your sister's phone. That's enough for now. Oh, and while we're there we will be taking their phones. I'll need you to text your sister's phone and see if anyone responds. If no one responds, it doesn't mean that they don't have anything to do with Andrea's murder, it just means that they're not the person texting you from your sister's phone. I need you to stay put at the police station while we get Wright and his wife. Don't do anything irrational, because if you do the chief will have me and Williams' heads, and all three of us won't be a part of the case anymore. You understand?"

"Yeah, I won't do anything stupid. So what do I tell the person tonight after the chief announces that the body found was my sister?"

"We'll cross that bridge when we get to it. C'mon we don't want to be late." Detective Stevenson grabbed her keys and headed for the door.

As they drove to the police station, both of them were quiet. Emily desperately wanted to go with Detective Williams and Detective Stevenson when they got Wright and his wife, but she was just happy to be a part of the interrogation. She realized that if Williams and Stevenson hadn't been the ones working on her sister's case, she probably wouldn't be a part of anything. When they finally arrived at the police station, Detective Williams had coffee and pastries ready for Emily, Detective Stevenson, and some other police officers who would be coming with them as they arrested Wright and his wife. As they walked in, Detective Williams was already telling the other police officers the plan.

"Alright everyone, since we haven't announced Andrea Kane's death I don't think we should have a problem arresting Wright and his wife and bringing them in for interrogation. Wright has been having some legal issues with his company, so he may think we're taking him in for questioning because of this. We'll allow him to think that either until he asks us why we're arresting him, or until we come in to interrogate him. The wife may be very cooperative, so we'll explain the situation to her once we arrive at her house. Officer Flores found that the last known message sent from Andrea's phone was sent from downtown on State Street. After that, nothing. It seems that the phone has been turned off."

"If we find that Nicholas and his wife aren't connected to this, we'll move on to Calvin Bruno and Lily Bostitch. We'll also check the camera footage in the area where the last message was sent," Detective Stevenson said. "Alright, everyone move out." As Detective Stevenson said this, everyone loaded into their cars to head to Nicholas Wright's home. Detective Williams and Detective Stevenson rode together as two police cars with two police officers each trailed behind them. When they arrived at Nicholas Wright's house in Lincoln Park, Detective Williams knocked on the door.

"This is Detective Williams and Detective Stevenson, I'm looking for Nicholas and Amber Wright," Detective Williams said authoritatively after knocking. Police officers surrounded the house in front and behind. A young woman who looked to be between the ages of 19 and 22 answered the door.

"Hi ma'am, I'm Detective Williams, and this is Detective Stevenson. We're looking for Amber and Nicholas Wright, are they home?" Detective Williams held up his badge.

"I'm their nanny, Dana. Mrs. Wright is home but not Nicholas," Dana said, frightened.

"May we please come in?" Detective Stevenson asked, moving closer to the door.

"Yes, I'll go grab Mrs. Wright." Dana opened the door for the detectives to come in. "I'll be right back. Kids, just finish eating your breakfast." Dana said to three children who were sitting at the counter eating their breakfast. One female child looked to be around five years old, one male child who looked to be nine years old, and another male child who looked to be thirteen years old.

“Dana, why are the police here?” the one who looked thirteen asked.

“I don’t know, just finish your breakfast while I grab your mother. The bus will be here soon to take you to school.” Dana ran upstairs to grab Mrs. Wright. The children just stared at the detectives, and the detectives waved at them.

“Maybe we shouldn’t arrest her while the kids are inside,” Detective Stevenson whispered, leaning over to Detective Williams.

“I was thinking the same thing,” he leaned over and whispered back. As he did this, Mrs. Wright came downstairs. She looked to be in her late 40’s or early 50’s. She was well dressed, her hair was perfectly done, and she looked confused but confident as she walked downstairs.

“Hi ma’am, are you Mrs. Wright?” Detective Williams asked.

“Yes, I’m Mrs. Wright. And you are?”

“I’m Detective Williams, and this is Detective Stevenson. We wanted to know if you could step outside so that we can tell you why we’re here.”

“Well why can’t you tell me inside the house?”

“We really don’t want to do this in front of your children,” Detective Williams whispered to the woman, and she looked confused and afraid.

“Dana, why don’t you get the children ready for school.”

“Mom, where are you going?” the boy who looked to be thirteen asked.

“Don’t worry, sweetheart, I just need to clear up some things about your father’s business with the detectives. Can we leave out the back, Detective? I don’t want my children or neighbors to see me leaving with you all,” Mrs. Wright whispered to Detective Williams.

“Sure,” Detective Williams whispered back. Then the school bus arrived for the kids.

“Let’s get you kids to school. Alright, get your things,” Dana said to the kids, and they all left out of the front door. Once the kids were outside and on the bus, the detectives walked out the back door with Mrs. Wright.

“I assume you all are here because of the legal issues my husband is having with his company? This is the third time this year that detectives have come by my home to take me in for questioning,” Mrs. Wright said as she and Detective Williams walked to the back of her house to put her in a police car so that they could head back to the police station.

"No ma'am, we're here about the dead body that was found at the construction site that your husband's construction company is working on," Detective Williams assured the woman.

"Well what does that have to do with me?" Mrs. Wright asked as Detective Williams beckoned her to get in the back of the police car.

"The dead body that was found has a connection to your husband," Detective Stevenson said.

"Why type of connection?" Mrs. Wright asked from the back of the police car.

"She was his sugar baby, and he was her sugar daddy," Detective Williams looked Mrs. Wright in the eyes to see if she knew anything about this. She tilted her head in disbelief. She pursed her lips, smirked a bit and shook her head. "Do you know where your husband is right now, ma'am?"

"He's at his office. I would advise you to take care of him before I do, Detective. Because once I take care of him, he won't have a penny left to his name. Can someone grab my bag out of the house for me please? It's on the counter. You can ask Dana to get it for me."

“Yes ma’am, I’ll have her grab it,” Detective Stevenson said as she headed back into the house and looked for Dana who was standing in the kitchen putting the children’s cereal bowls away.

“Dana, can you please hand me Mrs. Wright’s bag?” Detective Stevenson asked. Dana grabbed the bag and walked over to Detective Stevenson to hand it to her.

“Detective, is this about the dead body that was found at Nicholas’ construction site?”

“Yes, Dana, how did you know about that?”

“Nicholas and Mrs. Wright were talking about it, and I overheard. Do you know who it was?”

“Yes. I’m not at liberty to discuss that with you, but if you find anything suspicious just give me a call,” Detective Stevenson handed Dana her card.

“Okay, I will.” Detective Stevenson walked back to her squad car with Mrs. Wright’s bag in hand. Detective Williams sat in the car waiting for her.

“Was it me, or did she seem like she wasn’t shocked that he had a sugar baby?” Detective Williams said as Detective Stevenson entered the car and wrapped her seat belt around her.

"No, she didn't seem shocked at all. Let's go get Mr. Wright."

"I hope he is Mr. Right for this case," Detective Williams said as he drove off.

"Don't start with the dad jokes right now, Williams," Detective Stevenson texted Emily to tell her that they had Amber Wright. "I walked into that one, I should've just said Nicholas Wright. Dana knew about the dead body."

"The nanny? How did she know?"

"She knew that a dead body was found at the construction site. She overheard the Wrights talking about it."

"Okay, did she hear them say anything else about it?"

"She didn't say," Detective Stevenson said as she and Detective Williams kept driving until they reached Nicholas Wright's office. They walked in, and the receptionist asked if they had an appointment. Detective Williams and Stevenson just kept walking and held up their badges as they headed to Nicholas Wright's office door and opened it. When they arrived he was having a meeting. The detectives barged in with a couple police officers.

"What's going on?" Nicholas Wright asked in a tempered tone until he noticed who was standing in front of him. "Wait, aren't you the detectives who were investigating the dead body found at my construction site?"

"Yes, and it turns out that the dead body belonged to Andrea Kane," Detective Williams said as Nicholas Wright's face dropped. He paused for a moment, wondering how they found out about him and Andrea.

"I had nothing to do with that, Detectives," Nicholas Wright said, frightened.

"Well, regardless, we still need you to come with us for questioning. Let your friends know that you may have to reschedule this meeting, or not," Detective Stevenson said as she held up the handcuffs and arrest warrant for Nicholas Wright. Nicholas Wright stood with his mouth open.

"Nicholas?" one of the men at the table who was a part of the meeting said.

"I'm sorry everyone, we're going to have to reschedule the meeting," Nicholas Wright said as Detective Williams walked over to him to place the handcuffs on him.

"Until when?" One of the twelve people at the meeting asked.

“Um…I don’t know,” Nicholas Wright replied as he was handcuffed and Detective Williams escorted him out of the building into a police car. Detective Stevenson was beckoned by the receptionist to come over and talk.

“Detective, will Nicholas be gone for a while?” the receptionist asked as Detective Stevenson looked her up and down. “I’m Cynthia by the way.”

“It’s too early to tell,” Detective Stevenson responded. “Do you always refer to your boss by his first name?”

“We are really close, and he told me that I could.” Cynthia responded. She was a beautiful young girl who looked to be a bit older than Andrea. Detective Stevenson noticed that she blushed and smiled with this comment, and pushed her hair behind her ear. She could tell that Cynthia and Nicholas’ relationship traveled past the office.

“How long have you been working for Mr. Wright?” Detective Stevenson asked.

“For about six months now,” Cynthia responded.

“Has he mentioned anything about the dead body found at his construction site?” Detective Stevenson asked.

“No, not at all. I haven’t heard anything,” Cynthia said.

“Well, here’s my card in case you do. Let me know if you hear or find anything,” Detective Stevenson walked outside to the car where Detective Williams was sitting on the driver’s side.

“What happened back there?” Detective Williams asked.

“Nothing, receptionist seemed a bit worried about Mr. Wright, who she addresses by his first name,” Detective Stevenson responded.

“So you think they have a romantic relationship?” Detective Williams asked.

“Definitely, her body language suggested it. She looks a bit older than Andrea, and beautiful like her.”

“Do you think she could’ve had anything to do with Andrea being killed and her body being placed at the construction site?”

“I don’t know, it’s too early to tell. Besides, even if she had something to do with it we don’t have a warrant for her arrest. She also couldn’t have moved that body by herself.” Detective Stevenson rubbed her hand, stressed.

After their conversation, Detective Stevenson texted Emily to let her know that they arrested Nicholas Wright and his wife.

“Well, Nicholas seemed surprised when he heard Andrea Kane’s name,” Detective Williams said.

"Yeah, but he could just be surprised that we connected everything back to him," Detective Stevenson said.

"I guess we'll get some clues during the interrogation."

The detectives were finally back at the police station with Nicholas and Amber Wright in tow.

"NICHOLAS, I'M GOING TO KILL YOU," Amber Wright yelled once she entered the police station and saw Nicholas Wright's face. As she said this, he just held his head down. The police officers who traveled with the detectives placed the Wrights in two separate interrogation rooms. Once they were placed, the chief walked up to the detectives. The chief was a 5'6 man with a bloated beer belly and a receding hairline. Even though he was short and round, he commanded respect.

"You have them both?" the chief asked.

"Yeah, Chief, we got 'em," Detective Williams said.

"Chief, where is Emily Kane?" Detective Stevenson asked.

"The sister? I placed her in one of the interrogation rooms behind the window. She should be in the one that Nicholas Wright is in. I'll stand in there with her while you all interrogate him."

“Okay, so Williams, how do you want to tackle this? Do you want to ask them individually, or do you want to ask them together?” Detective Stevenson asked.

“We do this together, like we always do,” Detective Williams responded.

“Okay. Chief, let me talk to Emily Kane first. I want to get her prepared for everything she might hear,” Detective Stevenson said as she walked towards the interrogation room.

“Okay, lead the way,” the chief said as he and the two detectives walked into the interrogation room with Emily Kane. When they entered, Emily was happy to see Detective Stevenson.

“You got him?” Emily asked.

“I told you we would, and we got his wife too,” Detective Stevenson said, “We don’t have their devices just yet, we’ll need a warrant for that. But you can still text the number and see if they respond while we’re talking to them. We’ll talk to Nicholas first, then his wife. The chief will be standing in here with you while Williams and I are talking to Nicholas and his wife.”

“Okay, I’m ready. Do you really think he did it? He seems so sad,” Emily said as she looked at Nicholas’ face through the window.

"Don't let that face fool you. I've seen people commit heinous crimes and then look sad when we brought them in for questioning," Detective Stevenson said as Emily nodded her head.

"Alright Stevie, you ready?" Detective Williams asked Detective Stevenson.

"Yeah, let's go." They walked into the interrogation room with Nicholas Wright. He just sat there looking down, handcuffed, crying silently. Detective Stevenson and Williams sat down across from him.

"I didn't kill Andrea," Nicholas Wright said.

"We didn't say you did," Detective Williams said, leaning in towards Nicholas as he just kept shedding tears.

"But it is odd that you were one of her sugar daddies, and then she was found dead, frozen, and without a trace of blood at your construction site," Detective Stevenson said.

"Yeah, and another thing that's odd is the fact that Andrea Kane has been dead for almost two weeks — that's what her autopsy confirmed — and your company hasn't been able to work at that site for two weeks. Another thing that doesn't seem to make sense to me either, Mr. Wright, is the fact that you showed up to the crime scene the day we found Andrea Kane's body," Detective Williams said.

"I was there because my workers called me to tell me that there was a dead body at our construction site. I told you that," Nicholas Wright said, defending himself.

"We know, that's what you said when we saw you at the construction site a couple of days ago. But what confuses me is, why would your dead sugar baby's body be at your construction site?" Detective Stevenson said.

"You said it yourself, I wasn't Andrea's only sugar daddy. Maybe one of her other sugar daddies did it. Please, I didn't do this to her. I loved Andrea, I cared for her. I confided in her."

"Did you?" Detective Williams asked.

"Yes," Nicholas Wright responded.

"You cared for her so much that you would go for months without talking to her or seeing her?" Detective Stevenson asked.

"How do you know this?" Nicholas Wright asked, surprised.

"We have our sources. Did your wife know about her?" Detective Stevenson asked.

"Yeah, because she didn't seem too thrilled when we brought her in for questioning," Detective Williams said.

"I never really told Amber about Andrea."

"Here's what's bothering me: you're a 52-year-old man with a 48-year-old wife. You have three children, the number one construction company in Chicago, a nice house in Lincoln Park…" Detective Stevenson went on.

"Don't forget legal issues with his company," Detective Williams said.

"How did you think you were going to have time for a 20-year-old sugar baby? How did you think you were going to be able to keep it from your wife? Tell us, Mr. Wright. Your connection to this case depends on it."

"Okay, okay, I'll tell you everything. My wife had cheated on me with a younger man. She said it was because I wasn't spending enough time at home. I was always gone because I was working and focusing on the company. We've been getting a lot of competition in the past few years. I was trying to stay on top of everything and not have a failing business, but with keeping my business afloat, my marriage started sinking. My wife started cheating on me with her personal trainer. I came home early one day and found the two of them together. I was furious. He left, she and I started arguing, and I moved out that day. She didn't ask me to stay or anything, she was ready for me to go. She told me I was a horrible husband, and that all I did was work. So I left."

"You still haven't told us how you met Andrea Kane." Detective Stevenson didn't show Nicholas Wright any sympathy.

"I wasn't planning on becoming a 'sugar daddy,' but I wanted to get back at my wife, I guess. I didn't want anything serious, just someone to spend time with. I tried connecting with old flames from the past, but that didn't seem to work. I even tried those dating apps, but a lot of people I was meeting either wanted to get married or a one night stand. I didn't want marriage, I had already failed at that. I just wanted a girlfriend to throw in my wife's face to make her jealous. To make her feel how I felt. I confided in a friend of mine about it and they told me I should try this app for sugar daddies and sugar babies. I thought *What the heck?* You know, what do I have to lose? That's when I met Andrea. She was beautiful, fun, easy to be around. I didn't want anything serious and neither did she. I just wanted someone to spend time with, take a few pictures with, and to throw in my wife's face. I thought that's all I wanted, but as I started spending more time with Andrea I started to like her. I liked spending time with her. She was a good listener — I was at peace when I was around her. She just seemed to make all of my problems disappear."

"So why would you ghost her for months at a time?" Detective Stevenson asked.

"Because of things that I had to do with my kids and my business. I just didn't have as much time for her as she needed me to have. So I could only see her and spend time with her when I had it."

"I thought you said you never told your wife about Andrea? So how were you going to make her jealous?" Detective Stevenson asked.

"I never told her Andrea's name or that she was my sugar baby, but I showed her a picture of us when I took her to Las Vegas with me last year. I told her that this was my girlfriend and she went to Vegas with me."

"What did your wife say?" Detective Williams asked.

"You know what's crazy?" Nicholas Wright looked down at his cuffed hands sadly. "She didn't even care. When I showed her the picture she just said, 'Hope you had fun,' and shrugged her shoulders. She's one cold woman. I went through all of this just to make her upset and she didn't even care."

"Are you two still living separate lives or have you moved back home?" Detective Stevenson asked.

"I still have a place; my kids come over to see me. She hasn't filed for divorce."

"Yet. She hasn't filed for divorce yet," Detective Stevenson said as Nicholas Wright looked at her confused.

"She may have mentioned taking all your money when we placed her in our squad car today," Detective Williams explained.

"Do you think that there is the slightest chance that your wife might have been jealous of Andrea?"

"She didn't seem like it, but even if she was, she wouldn't have killed Andrea. She didn't know her to kill her. This is all my fault, I shouldn't have ever gotten on that app."

"Andrea Kane was last seen on January 28th, and she died either on that day or on the 29th. When do you last remember seeing her?" Detective Stevenson asked, leaning forward towards Nicholas Wright.

"I hadn't seen Andrea since December 23rd when we met at a hotel for dinner and I gave her a Christmas gift. I gave her a handbag and a wallet."

"And where were you on January 28th and the 29th?" Detective Williams asked.

"I had to go to court on the 29th because of the legal issues that I'm having with my company. On the night of the 29th, a friend of mine had a get-together at his house, and I went. On the 28th, my son had a volleyball game. My family and I went to his game, and then we went out to dinner that night."

"Can you give us the name of the friend who had the get-together on the 29th?" Detective Williams asked.

"Michael Gordon."

"So the last time you saw Andrea was December 23rd? You didn't take her to Florida with you recently?" Detective Stevenson asked.

"No Detective, I haven't been to Florida recently. I don't know where you're getting this from. I haven't seen Andrea since December 23rd."

"When was the last time you spoke to her?" Detective Stevenson asked.

"You know what's crazy? I wasn't expecting you to say that Andrea Kane was dead. Because she texted me four days ago." As

Nicholas Wright gave this last statement the detectives looked at each other in shock.

"What did the text message say?" Detective Williams asked.

"She asked me if I wanted to go out to dinner. I said I couldn't because I promised my kids I would take them to a Bull's game. When I said this, she didn't respond."

"Alright then, we'd like a copy of your phone records and I'm going to check in the system, contact your alibi, and see if your stories check out for the 28th and the 29th," Detective Williams said.

"Am I free to go?" Nicholas Wright asked.

"Not quite yet. I also want to talk to ask the people who live and work close by your construction site and see if they saw you there any time in the past couple of weeks when Andrea was dead," Detective Stevenson said.

"Well because of the legal issues, me and my crew weren't allowed to be at the construction site. That was a court order."

"Well you know how rules work, Mr. Wright. Some people feel like they're meant to be broken. Now if you'll excuse us, we're going to go talk to your wife," Detective Stevenson said as she and Detective

Williams stood up to go into the interrogation room where Amber Wright was sitting.

"I'll have Officer Flores look into these alibis, and Officer Hunt can go by the site and ask people if they remember seeing Mr. Wright around there. I'll have Officer Grant get a copy of the phone records for me," the chief told the detectives as he and Emily exited from behind the window of Nicholas Wright's interrogation room.

"So he's been getting the text messages from Andrea's phone too?" Emily asked as she ran behind the chief.

"We'll have to see once we get the phone records. Did you text Andrea's number to see if you got a response?" Detective Stevenson asked.

"Yeah, I asked where she was, and the person just said that they were with Calvin again for breakfast. Then they were going to go shopping."

"Okay, so whoever has the phone, it isn't the Wrights," Detective Williams said.

"But that still doesn't clear their names. Let's go talk to Mrs. Wright," Detective Stevenson said as she and Williams headed to the interrogation room where Amber Wright was sitting. The chief and

Emily stood behind the window again. Amber Wright just sat in her seat. Instead of crying like her husband, she sat with her head held high, a pompous look on her face, one eye brow raised, lips pursed, and her hands in her lap.

“Hands on the table, please,” Detective Williams said as they entered the interrogation room and sat down.

“Is all of this really necessary? Why would I kill my husband’s, who I am separated from, sugar baby? If I could kill anyone, it would be him,” Amber Wright said, rolling her eyes.

“Nicholas told us that you two were separated,” Detective Stevenson said.

“Exactly, so why am I still here?”

“Because we still have a few questions to ask you connected to Andrea Kane’s death,” Detective Williams said.

“Look my condolences go out to this young lady and her family, but I don’t care anything about this case, Nicholas, and whoever Nicholas is with.”

“So you weren’t at all jealous of the relationship your husband had with this 20-year-old woman?” Detective Williams.

“Jealous? Don’t be absurd. Why would I be jealous of this young woman?” Amber Wright smirked.

“Because she was young, beautiful, and she was sleeping with your husband?” Detective Williams said.

“Oh, please. Why would I be jealous of someone who wants what I have?”

“What do you mean by that, Mrs. Wright?” Detective Stevenson asked.

“That girl, rest her soul, was with Nicholas for his money. I already have his money. My father has money as well. Nicholas gives me whatever I want just so that I won’t divorce him and really take everything he has. That may all change soon. She wanted a nice car, a nice place, shoes, handbags, jewelry, trips, and clothes, all of which I have. I mean, she was a sugar baby, of course that’s what she wanted from him. And from the picture that he showed me of them in Vegas, if I remember correctly, I could tell she was a beautiful young woman. Too good-looking for Nicholas.”

“So when he showed you the picture you weren’t the slightest bit jealous?” Detective Stevenson said.

"Pleeease. I knew from taking one look at that girl that she was only with Nicholas for his money. He seemed like he was upset because I wasn't jealous."

"Were you not jealous because you had someone as well?" Detective Williams asked.

"Maybe. He told you he caught me fooling around with my personal trainer? He's 25," Amber Wright smiled.

"Hey may have mentioned it," Detective Stevenson said.

"Why would I be jealous of his sugar baby when I had a big, strong, young man to spend time with?"

"He told us that he started talking to Andrea to get back at you for cheating on him with your personal trainer. He said you cheated first," Detective Williams said.

"Really?" Amber Wright was shocked. "Ha."

"Is that not true?" Detective Stevenson asked.

"Sweetheart, I've lost count how many times Nicholas has cheated on me. Ever since he started making more money with his construction company, which has been for the past 15 years of our marriage, he's been cheating. I'd be shocked if this girl, Andrea Kane, was the only girl he's been with since he started talking to her."

"So, he's had multiple infidelities and multiple girlfriends?" Detective Williams asked.

"Yes, and I have had multiple infidelities and boyfriends as well."

"Well, why was he so upset about your personal trainer?" Detective Stevenson asked.

"Because he found us together, and because we were at the house. Nicholas is all about saving face. He felt that someone might have seen Daniel — that's my young man's name — come in. He didn't want anybody finding out. I've never had one of my flings at the house and neither has he. But Daniel was my personal trainer, so he was over often."

"So you don't think Nicholas was jealous of you and… Daniel?" Detective Stevenson asked.

"Not at all, he just didn't want anyone knowing about us."

"Mrs. Wright, why have you and Mr. Wright stayed together all this time?" Detective Williams asked.

"For the company and for our children. My father invested a nice amount of money in Nicholas' construction company. My father has a big law firm here in Chicago. He never liked Nicholas, but he believed in his idea about the construction company. He invested in his company. If we ever broke up, he would take Nicholas for everything he has. Even though we are still together, and we hate each other, we have an amicable separation for our children. If I divorce Nicholas, and my father takes everything he has, I fear that it would be horrible for our children. They think we've just had a long fight, but they've never met anyone we're seeing. Family is important to both of us, and we don't want to jeopardize that."

"That's very decent of you both," Detective Williams said. "I have a few more questions for you. Andrea Kane has been dead for almost two weeks now. Her autopsy revealed that she died January 28th or 29th. Where were you both those days?"

"Well, Nicholas had a court day on the 29th, so I was in court with him. I'm part owner of the construction company so I had to be there."

"Oh, that's a detail he left out," Detective Stevenson said.

"He always leaves that detail out," Amber Wright said. "Anyway, that was during the day and then in the afternoon I had lunch with Daniel. After that, it was time for the kids to come home, so I went home with the kids and Dana. I had dinner with them. On the morning of the 28th I had to get my son ready for a volleyball game. Then we went to his game, and then we went out for dinner. Dana came back later on that night, and then I spent the night with Daniel once my kids were asleep."

"Well, we'll check into all of this. Thank you Mrs. Wright," Detective Williams said.

"Mhhhhmmm. Now can I go? And where is my bag?"

Detectives Williams and Stevenson walked out of the interrogation room and went behind the window with the chief and Emily.

"So how do you two feel?" the chief asked.

"I don't know, I have a funny feeling neither one of them did it," Detective Williams said.

"Yeah, same," Detective Stevenson said, closing the door behind her.

"But then why would my sister's body be at their construction site? It doesn't make any sense — it has to connect to them somehow."

"I don't know, that's what's bothering me. I don't feel like they did this, but why leave her body at their site? I don't feel like that's a coincidence," Detective Stevenson said.

"Well, I'll check their alibis for you two. I'll be giving my speech to the media about Andrea's death at 5:00 pm. In the meantime, I think you should get back to Nicholas and ask him why he failed to mention that his wife is part owner of the construction company and that they each have had multiple infidelities in their marriage." The chief exited the room.

"Okay, Chief," Detective Williams said.

"Wait, do you think that Amber Wright did this to frame Nicholas Wright?" Emily asked. "She really seemed adamant about taking more of his money. Maybe if this gets out in the media, she'd have a reason to divorce him?"

"No, Emily, because then their kids would know, and I don't think Amber wants that for their kids," Detective Stevenson assured Emily.

"Yeah, and if it ever came out that Nicholas Wright killed someone, their construction company would cease to exist even if Amber Wright and her father were the owners. It would be sketchy, especially knowing that a dead body was found, and it was the body of his sugar baby," Detective Williams said.

"Yeah, they're too invested. It can't be them, but we better get back in and ask why he didn't mention those details." Detective Stevenson and Detective Williams exited and went back into the interrogation room with Nicholas Wright.

"Did my alibis check out?" Nicholas asked.

"Not yet, we have some more questions to ask you. Why didn't you tell us that your wife was part owner of your construction company?" Detective Stevenson asked.

"And why didn't you tell us about the multiple infidelities between you and your wife?" Detective Williams asked.

"Yeah, you made it seem as if you became jealous that she cheated on you so you cheated on her to make her jealous," Detective Stevenson said.

"I didn't mention that she was part owner of the construction company because I never mention that to anyone. When her father invested in my company, the only way he would do it was if Amber became part owner. I didn't want this, but I had no other option. I needed his money to start my company. And yes, we have had multiple infidelities, but I didn't say anything about them because they have nothing to do with this case. I started dating Andrea after the incident with my wife and her trainer. Even though we both have had many infidelities, we've never had a true relationship with those partners. It was like they didn't matter, but we mattered to each other. She was and still is in a relationship with her trainer. So I wanted to show her that I had a relationship too, even though I really didn't want one. I was being a bit childish and petty, but regardless of that, I didn't kill Andrea. Like I said, I cared for her. And whenever I didn't have time to be with her she didn't push, and she never became angry, she understood that I was busy. I hope you all find out who did this to her."

"Let's hope so, for your sake," Detective Williams said.

After Nicholas Wright said these words, both detectives left his interrogation room to get coffee. A couple of hours had passed before the chief finally came to the detectives.

"All alibis check out, they're free to go. And we checked the camera footage from the area where the last message was sent from Andrea's phone. It was a dead end, a bunch of people texting from their phones walking down the street. It could be anyone, especially because it's cold here in Chicago, and everyone is bundled up and masked because of the pandemic. So you can't even see people's faces or bodies. I think trying to track the phone's location may not be the best way to solve this case, but we'll keep using it," the chief said.

"Okay, that makes sense, Chief. All of this still doesn't explain how the body got to their construction site," Detective Stevenson said.

"I don't know either, but they don't seem to be the killers. I'll make my announcement tonight, but tomorrow morning be ready bright and early to interrogate the second sugar daddy and his girlfriend. Oh, and don't expect to get them in your hands so easily. They may end up finding out about Andrea Kane on the news tonight, and we don't have a warrant yet for their arrest."

"How you feel?" Detective Williams asked Detective Stevenson.

"Like we've hit a wall. I thought for sure we'd get some information that would lead us closer to knowing who killed Andrea. It's just not adding up; Andrea was Nicholas' sugar baby, her dead body was found at Nicholas' construction site, and the wife knew about her, but neither of them are responsible for her death."

"I know, but we've seen crazier incidents." Detective Williams sipped his coffee.

"WILLIAMS, STEVENSON, GET IN THERE AND LET THOSE PEOPLE OUT," the chief yelled from his office.

“Let’s go,” Detective Stevenson said as she rolled her eyes and hung her head down, defeated.

“Your alibi checks out,” Detective Stevenson said as she opened the door to Nicholas Wright’s interrogation room. “You’re free to go.”

“Thank you,” Nicholas said, holding up his hands so he could be uncuffed. Detective Stevenson walked over with the key to uncuff him. “I hope you find out who did this to Andrea. She was a good person, she didn’t deserve this.”

“I intend to.” Nicholas Wright walked out. Meanwhile, Detective Williams was informing Amber Wright that her alibis had checked out.

“You’re free to go.”

“Of course. I knew it wouldn’t be long. I told you I didn’t do anything.” Amber Wright held up her hands to grab her bag from Detective Williams. “I really do hope you find out who murdered this girl.”

“You care that much about her?” Detective Williams asked as he handed Amber Wright her bag.

"Not just her, I'm for any woman doing what she has to do to make her money. No one should ever take that away from her," Amber Wright said. "You know, you're cute too."

"I'm married with twin boys, ma'am," Detective Williams responded.

"Well, can't blame a girl for trying. All of the good ones are taken. Your wife is a lucky woman," Amber Wright said as she began to exit the interrogation room.

"No, I'm the lucky one." Detective Williams smiled.

"Good answer," Amber Wright said. Once he was done, Detective Williams went on the other side of the interrogation room with Detective Stevenson and Emily.

"So what now?" Emily asked. "It seems like we're back where we started."

"Emily, I told you these things take time. Tomorrow we'll talk to Calvin Bruno and Lily Bostitch."

"And what if they didn't do it either?"

"Then we move on to Albert and Samantha Little," Detective Williams responded, trying to comfort Emily.

"And, what if it's not them either?"

“Then we’ll look for more clues. Don’t worry, we’ll figure out who did this to your sister,” Detective Stevenson said.

“I just — I just thought we’d get more information today. I, um…I need to go call Mama Kim back. She called me while you were interrogating Wright and his wife. She’s probably worried sick about me.” Emily exited the interrogation room.

“Poor kid,” Detective Williams said.

“I know,” Detective Stevenson said.

“You don’t think all of this is too much for her?”

“I do, but she wants to be a part of this. If I told her to step back she would probably do something crazy but still try to find a way to be a part of the case.”

“Well, it’s 12:30, and I’m starving. You want to grab some lunch together?”

“No, you go ahead. I need time to wrap my mind around all this.”

“Alright, I’ll grab you something anyway,” Detective Williams smirked as they walked ahead.

“Thanks,” Detective Stevenson said, as Detective Williams opened the door so they could go out into the hallway. Both detectives stepped outside in front of the police station. They saw Emily on the phone.

"No, Mama Kim, I'm fine. I'm at the police station. They've interrogated the man and his wife who own the construction company that was working on the construction site where Dre was found dead."

"Stevie, I'm going to get lunch, I'll see you later." Detective Williams walked away.

"Mama Kim, I'm fine. I'm staying with a friend, I'm okay. Mama Kim, you know I can't come to your house. I'll stop by later on today, bye." Emily hung up the phone.

"She wants you to come home with her?" Detective Stevenson asked.

"Yeah, but I don't want to go over there today. She knows I can't come there and stay. I know she's worried, I just can't go over there right now."

"So what do you want to do?"

"I don't know, I'm just so upset right now."

"Hey, maybe we should go somewhere just you and I."

"Where?"

After a long drive, Detective Stevenson and Emily had finally reached their destination. Detective Stevenson had taken Emily to a go-kart riding place out in the suburbs of Illinois. Emily was shocked to see that Detective Stevenson had brought her here.

"A go-kart riding place?" Emily asked, confused, as she unbuckled her seat belt.

"Yeah," Detective Stevenson responded.

"Why?"

"Whenever I have a rough day and just need to let everything go, I come here. I ride around the track a few times and forget about my worries"

"So not hitting something, not playing basketball, not getting ice cream go-kart riding?"

"Don't knock it 'til you try it. Now come on, I need this and you need this." Detective Stevenson opened the door for Emily as they entered the go-kart riding place.

"Okay, anything to take my mind off of what happened today." They waited in line until it was their turn. They finally reached the front of the counter.

“Hey Detective, how you doin’?” the man behind the counter asked Detective Stevenson.

“I’m fine, and yourself?”

“I am wonderful. Who is your friend?”

“This is Emily, and we’re both in desperate need of a drive. Two people for three laps.”

“Ooooh, sounds like y’all had a rough day.”

“Yeah, it was.”

“Okay, here you go.” The man behind the counter handed Detective Stevenson and Emily helmets.

“So what made you get into go-kart riding?” Emily asked as they walked to their go-karts.

“I would go go-kart riding with my dad and brothers back in Alabama. I looked for a place when I came to Chicago, but I found this one. It’s in the suburbs, so a bit further out. Even though it’s further out, I love coming here. When I first became a detective, I needed something to take my mind off of everything. Some people played basketball, went to eat, went out for drinks, things like that, but go-kart riding was my thing. Sometimes I like doing things by myself, and many of my colleagues weren't into go-kart riding. So this was one thing that I could do alone."

"Cool, well I guess, if I like it you won't have to go alone anymore," Emily said.

"You ready?" Detective Stevenson asked.

"Yeah, let's go for it." Emily smiled.

Both ladies sat in their small go-karts, helmets on, hands on the wheel. They glanced at one another and looked at the lights as they changed from red, to yellow, to green. They sped across the track turn after turn after turn. As they were going around the track Emily started to understand why Detective Stevenson did this. It was relaxing, and she started to let everything go. As she sped and turned, everything just seemed to fade away. Everything that she was worried about, the feeling of loneliness, the anxiety from her sister's murder case, the shame of her mother, it all faded away. When Detective Stevenson and Emily completed their three laps, they finished up at the go-kart riding place and headed back into Detective Stevenson's car.

"So how'd it feel?"

"I felt what you were talking about. I felt like I had let everything go."

"See what I mean? It's 3 o'clock. We should be back at my place just in time for the chief to make his announcement on the news about your sister."

"Okay, then we can text the number and see what the person on the other end has to say? "

"No, not yet," Detective Stevenson said.

"No? Why not?" Emily asked.

"I thought about it, while we were driving. Don't say anything, just wait until they mention it to you. Let them tell you that they know, that you know, that Andrea is dead."

"But what if they keep lying?"

"Then keep going along with the lie. Let's see how long they'll lie. Who knows, maybe they'll say the right thing that'll give us a clue of who they are."

"Okay. I'm going to lean back and go to sleep. I didn't get any sleep last night. I was too anxious about today."

"Okay, I'll wake you up once we get to my place."

After almost two hours, Emily and Detective Stevenson finally arrived at Detective Stevenson's condo. They pulled into the garage of her condo building.

"Alright Emily, wake up, we're here."

"What time is it?"

"It's 4:58, so we'd better hurry. The chief will be making his announcement in a couple minutes. Let's hurry." Both of them exited the car and ran to the elevator.

"Wait, you don't have a television, how are we going to watch his announcement?"

"Oh, I have a small television in my room. You haven't been in there, so you haven't seen it." Detective Stevenson unlocked the door to her condo. "Alright, turn on the television in my room."

"What channel is he on?"

"He's on channel seven news."

"He's on."

"Okay, turn it up."

The chief made his announcement on the news. He informed the press Andrea's body had been found at a construction site underneath ten bags of cement mix. He mentioned that she had been shot four times, which was her cause of death, that she had been frozen, and possibly transported. He mentioned that they had brought suspects in for questioning, but they had alibis and were no longer in police custody. He ended by saying the detectives working on the case would bring more suspects in tomorrow for questioning.

"Wow! It feels good to know that it's finally out," Emily said.

Ring. Ring. Ring.

"Hold on, that's me," Detective Stevenson said. "Hello, this is Detective Stevenson."

"Hi, this is Dana, the Wrights' nanny."

"Hi Dana, is everything okay?"

"Well, Mrs. Wright came home and told me everything about what happened with that poor girl. She told me that's why you brought them in for questioning. I also saw the chief of police announce it on the news just now."

"Thanks Dana, is there anything you wanted to tell me?"

"It's just that, I feel bad and I overheard the Wright's arguing about their significant others today when they got home. Nicholas was upset a while back when he found out about Mrs. Wright's boyfriend and he told her that he would be willing to give up everyone else if she gave up her boyfriend."

"And?"

"She said she wouldn't do it. I didn't know he was talking about Andrea Kane. Nicholas has had many girlfriends in my time working here. I don't think he'd kill anyone. Although, before the trial date, he did say he had done something stupid. I overheard him and Mrs. Wright talking. I thought he was just talking about everything with his construction company, but maybe he was talking about Andrea Kane."

"Dana, what are you trying to tell me?"

"I'm saying maybe he had someone to kill Andrea Kane. You know, like a hit man."

"What would his motive be?" Detective Stevenson asked.

"I don't know, but I'll try asking Mrs. Wright more questions. When she gets drunk she tells me everything."

"If you're willing to do that, I'm fine with that. See what you can find, just don't get yourself hurt. And thank you, Dana."

"No problem. I hope I can find something. Mrs. Wright told me they both had alibis and that the only connection they had to the case was Andrea's dead body being found at their construction site. Also,

Nicholas was her sugar daddy, which I didn't know. Other than that, they're not connected to her death."

"Sounds like she told you everything. Well, thank you, Dana. Call me if you hear anything else."

"Will do." Dana hung up the phone.

"Who was that?" Emily asked.

"The Wrights' nanny, she says she thinks that maybe Nicholas Wright had a hit put out on Andrea. But she doesn't have any evidence to support that. So she says she's going to try to get some more information out of Amber Wright by getting her drunk," Detective Stevenson explained to Emily.

"Why does she think that if she has no evidence?"

"Because she overheard them arguing about Amber's boyfriend, and Nicholas said he'd be willing to drop all of his girlfriends. He has many, it turns out, and his wife mentioned that too. Before they went to court, the nanny also overheard him say that he had done something stupid. She thought he was talking about some legal issues with his construction company, but she thinks now he may have been talking about Andrea."

"How do you feel?"

“I don’t think they’re connected to your sister’s death besides her body being found. I’ll listen to what Dana has to say and keep the Wrights in mind because she was found at their construction site. But I don’t think it’s them.”

“Well, I’m with you. I trust you,” Emily said, smiling and reassuring Detective Stevenson that she knew everything would be okay.

“Thanks, I think the nanny is just shaken up by everything and wants to help. Tomorrow we’ll talk to Calvin and Lily. Hopefully that leads us closer to something.”

Ring. Ring. Ring.

“Let me take this Emily,” Detective said as she answered the phone again. “Hello?”

“Hi, this is Cynthia, the receptionist from Nicholas’ office.”

“Hi Cynthia, how are you? Thanks for contacting me,” Detective Stevenson said.

“I just watched the news, I’m sorry to hear about the girl who died…I mean who was murdered. I just wanted to tell you that I don’t believe Nicholas would do anything like that.”

“Why is that?” Detective Stevenson asked.

"I know Nicholas, he's a good man. His wife on the other hand, is a terror to be around. She's cut-throat, conniving, and vicious. She should be considered a suspect…" Cynthia began saying before Detective Stevenson cut her off.

"Cynthia, do you have any evidence to support this statement?"

"Not much, just her character."

"I understand Mrs. Wright may not be the nicest person, but why would Mrs. Wright kill Andrea Kane? How would she know her?" Detective Stevenson asked.

"I don't know, but Mrs. Wright is sketchy and evil. I saw when you all left with Nicholas today that she was in the back of one of the squad cars. She's part owner of the company, and I overheard her and Nicholas arguing loudly one day when I came back to the office to grab my keys after I had left. They argued about their infidelities, the financial stability of the company, getting a divorce, and Mrs. Wright said she'll take Nicholas for everything he has. I think she's trying to tear him down and keep the company for her and her father. This is just a speculation, I know, but I think this is a plot by Mrs. Wright to tear Nicholas down for good."

"Cynthia, that still doesn't explain how Andrea's body was found at the construction site?" Detective Stevenson asked.

"Well, maybe she owed them money, or maybe she was one of Nicholas' girlfriends, I don't know. But I'll let you know if I find anything."

"Thank you, Cynthia," Detective Stevenson said before she hung up the phone.

"Now who was that?" Emily asked.

"The receptionist, she says she thinks it's Mrs. Wright and not Nicholas," Detective Stevenson said. "I think it's only because she has a romantic relationship with Nicholas."

"How do you know?" Emily asked.

"Because of her body language." Detective Stevenson responded.

"Do you think she's a suspect?"

"Too early to tell, and too early to get a warrant for her and connect her to anything. You should get some sleep, we have to do this all over again tomorrow."

Chapter 5 - Calvin Bruno & Lily Bostitch

It was 7:00 am on February 11th. The morning after the chief had announced that the body found at the construction site was Andrea Kane. Emily woke up to find her phone flooded with text messages and missed calls from people who wanted to give their condolences, or ask if what they saw on the news was true. Emily didn't respond to any of the text messages, voicemails, or missed calls. In her mind, she was done crying, she didn't feel like hearing other people cry, and she didn't want to explain the story, the case, her whereabouts, or anything to anyone. She just kept lying on Detective Stevenson's couch staring at the ceiling and letting her mind race with thoughts about her sister. She hoped and prayed that Calvin and Lily would be able to give some kind of information that would help the detectives find Andrea's killer. She thought of conversations with her sister.

Maybe there was something Andrea had said or something she could remember that could be a clue to solving the mystery of who killed her sister.

"Emily…Emily…EMILY," Detective Stevenson yelled as she came out of her bedroom fully dressed with her badge and gun ready. "It's time to get up and get ready. We have to try to interrogate Calvin Bruno and Lily Bostitch."

"What do you mean, try?"

"Well, besides the information you gave us, Calvin and Lily don't have a big connection to this case. Even though the information you gave was helpful, and we wouldn't be this far this quickly without it, Calvin and Lily aren't huge suspects just because he was one of your sister's sugar daddies. Nicholas and Amber own the construction company that works at the construction site where your sister's dead body was found, and he was one of your sister's sugar daddies. They were the prime suspects. So we may not get anything out of Calvin and Lily today."

"Wait, I thought you had a warrant for their arrest?"

"No, we had a warrant for Nicholas Wright, not Calvin and Lily. They can say that they want a lawyer present, which they have the right to do, and their lawyer could advise them not to speak. I just want to prepare you for the worst, that's why I'm telling you this. The only reason we're even questioning them is because of your statement that your sister was on her way to see Calvin the day she died. So Calvin is the last known person who saw your sister before she died."

"And what about Lily Bostitch?"

"It was only because of her connection to Calvin and her anger at finding out about your sister that she may be a suspect. We found out that Calvin and Lily are living together in a loft in the South Loop area. For this interrogation, we won't have to take them into custody, but maybe we can get some answers from them if we go by their place and interrogate them there."

"Okay, so what do you need me to do?"

"Well, I felt like you may need some comfort because of the announcement, so I didn't do any digging on our suspects for today. I had Williams look into Calvin Bruno and Lily Bostitch last night. I wanted him to see if he could find anything so we could try to get a warrant for their arrest. We'll stop by the station first to see what Williams found. If we're lucky, we'll have a warrant and we can bring them both in. If we're semi-lucky, we'll have a warrant for Calvin

Bruno, bring him in, and then figure out what to do about Lily Bostitch. If we're not lucky, we'll just stop by their home and ask questions."

"Why would that be unlucky?"

"Because we wouldn't have a home court advantage. Without a warrant, Calvin and Lily can easily say they don't know anything about Andrea Kane, and it would be your word against theirs. We also don't have Andrea's phone or any pictures of her and Calvin together…" Detective Stevenson went on.

"I do have pictures of them together. Dre would send me pictures of them when they went on trips together. And I have screenshots of the text messages Lily sent Calvin about Dre."

"Emily, why didn't you show me this before?"

"Well, it's only been a couple days since my sister died. I didn't think about it. I've also been trying to get past my grief and think of anything that Dre told me or showed me that might be evidence too. And I gave you guys access to my phone records, so I thought you may be able to see all of that."

"You're right, I'm sorry. You are grieving, and thanks for trying to think of more information. Well, we do have your phone records,

Williams looked into those as well. He'll be able to tell us some new information today. Can you think of anyone else who Andrea may have talked to about her time with her sugar daddies? Maybe they'll have some insight."

"The only other people are her friends, Veronica and Riley."

"Okay, if we don't get any closer to finding any clues, maybe we can see if Riley and Veronica are open to talking. Have they contacted you? I heard your phone going off all night, but I saw that you didn't answer."

"Yeah, I'm sure they've contacted me. I didn't answer because I didn't feel like speaking to anyone. I'll reach out to them and see if they want to share anything. Do you want me to try texting my sister's number today?"

"We'll see how things are going with Calvin and Lily first. Then you can text your sister's phone and once the person texts you back we'll know that it's not either of them who has your sister's phone. We'll have to wait to see how all of this goes. We could just reach a dead end today."

"Okay, I'm ready."

"Uh, no you're not. You still need to shower and get dressed."

"Oh, yeah. Do you have something else for me to wear?"

"Already in the bathroom on the counter. Hurry, we don't want to be late." Emily rushed to the bathroom to get ready. She showered so quickly she barely felt clean, but she didn't want to waste any time. She hoped Detective Williams had found something last night that might lead them a bit closer to her sister's killer. She jumped out of the shower, hopped into the clothes that Detective Stevenson had set out for her, and stood in front of the mirror. She hadn't really looked at herself in a mirror for the past couple of weeks. Her hair was a mess, her nails were bitten low, her face was dry, her eyes were swollen from crying, and her bangs needed cutting. She rolled up her sleeve and looked at the tattoo on her wrist, the matching tattoo that she and Andrea had. The tattoo was a cat holding a cookie; a lot of people didn't understand it, but that's why she and Andrea got it. It was an inside thing between the two of them. Their grandmother used to call them cat and cookie. Andrea was the cat because she was wild and untamed. Emily was the cookie because she was sweet but with a hard outer shell. She felt herself starting to cry again, but instead of shedding tears she pulled down her sleeve, put her hair into a ponytail, and opened the bathroom door.

"Do you have any lotion I can put on my face?" Emily asked Detective Stevenson as she exited the bathroom.

"Yeah, it's in my room on my dresser."

"Thanks," Emily went into Detective Stevenson's room and grabbed the lotion. While there she saw a file on the dresser with her sister's name on it. She wanted to look inside it and see what was rolling around in the detectives' heads, but she knew that it was time for her to go.

"Emily, you ready?" Detective Stevenson yelled from the living room that was only steps away.

"Yeah, coming." Emily quickly rubbed the lotion on her face, left Detective Stevenson's room, and headed for the door. Both of them rushed to the elevator, went into the parking garage attached to Detective Stevenson's condo building, entered the car, and sped to the police station.

While in the car Detective Stevenson asked,
"Hey, when do you have to go back to school?"

"Oh, I'll email my professors and let them know my sister died," Emily said looking down at her feet.

"Okay, because I don't want you to miss classes because you're focused on this case. This is for me and Williams to figure out, not you. You have to get done with school."

"But if I go to school, all I'm going to be thinking about is the case, texting my sister's phone, and figuring out who murdered her. I won't get much from the lessons anyway. Besides, since the pandemic, my professors put stuff online as well. I can hop on there tonight and see what I missed. Everything is pretty easy for me, so I'm sure I can get it done quickly."

"Okay, but get on it soon. And let me know if you need anything."

"Thanks, but you have my sister's case to worry about, remember? I don't want anything distracting you from that." Detective Stevenson glanced at Emily, wondering when she became so demanding. The ladies finally pulled up to the police station. Both Emily and Detective Stevenson exited the car, hoping Williams had found some piece of the puzzle that they could use for Andrea's case. As they walked into the police station, they stopped at Williams' desk and just stared at him, waiting for him to respond.

"We have the warrant for Calvin Bruno," Detective Williams said as both ladies breathed a big sigh of relief.

"How did you get it?" Detective Stevenson asked.

"I looked over the phone records Emily gave us. Not only was Andrea's relationship with Calvin a red flag, but him being the person she was supposed to see the day of her death was as well. Then I found this in Emily's text exchanges with Andrea," Detective Williams said, pulling out a copy of Emily's phone records and circling the text message exchanges from Andrea. "Right here, last summer before she died, she mentions that Calvin grabbed her and pushed her up against the wall so she wouldn't leave. She texted you and said she was trying to leave because Lily had texted Calvin and told him that she saw him and Andrea going into a hotel together. Then she stated that as she was trying to leave, Calvin got all hysterical and told her to stay put. She said she was afraid of him at that moment and afraid to leave."

"I remember that day now. I called her after that □ she was crying, and I told her that she should leave. She said Calvin came back into the room and apologized. When she came home a couple days later, she said everything was fine between them, but he probably couldn't see her for a while until Lily calmed down a bit. All of that happened over the summer," Emily said.

"So because of this physical altercation, I was able to make a connection to the bruises on Andrea's body. Maybe she was afraid of Calvin, maybe he could have had violent episodes. I know you didn't mention this Emily, and I thought it may have been a stretch, but it was enough to get us a warrant. Especially since Andrea's death looks to be a domestic homicide."

"Williams, you're brilliant," Detective Stevenson said.

"I know. I also found this on Lily Bostitch's TikTok." Detective Williams pulled up a video of Lily saying that she couldn't believe Calvin had cheated on her and that she saw him going into a hotel with another woman. She said she wanted to kill him. She stated that all girls know the code and that it's wrong for a woman to sleep with another woman's man. She said she would expose the woman he was going into the hotel with to the world.

"Wait, she posted that? Wouldn't something personal like that jeopardize her job and Calvin's?"

"Stevenson, have you seen what people post on the internet now? This wouldn't jeopardize anything. She didn't say how she would do it; she could have meant that she would show Andrea's picture on TikTok or find out who she was and tell everyone about her. It didn't have to mean death. I didn't get a warrant for her arrest for this. I'm hoping that Calvin may say something that we can use against Lily that would help us to get a warrant for her."

"Okay, but in the meantime, I have an idea. When we go to arrest Calvin this morning, we can ask Lily if she would like to come in for questioning, which may help to clear Calvin's name. If she chooses to come in, we have her right where we want her."

"That works too," Detective Williams said. "Emily, you're awfully quiet."

"Oh, I'm just watching you guys figure everything out," Emily responded.

"Well you look a lot better today, I hope you got some rest after the announcement," Detective Williams said.

"Not really. My phone has been ringing like crazy," Emily said.

"Did anyone text you from your sister's number?" Detective Williams asked.

"Not yet. I told her that we would text the number when we're questioning Calvin and Lily and see if someone responds. That way we'll know that it's not the two of them who have Andrea's phone," Detective Stevenson said.

"Okay. Emily, I had a question for you as well. You've been driving your sister's car for the past couple of weeks. I thought you said that her sugar daddies didn't know where she lived. So why didn't she take her car to go see Calvin?" Detective Williams asked as Detective Stevenson just squinted her eyes at him, wondering why he was asking Emily this.

"Oh, Andrea took an Uber to go see Calvin that morning. I had class as well, so she let me use the car to go to school. She would do that sometimes when I had class, but none of them knew where she stayed. At least, I don't think they did."

"Okay, that makes sense. Alright Emily, Stevenson and I are going to head to Calvin Bruno's place. Hopefully he's still there and not gone to his office or anything, and we'll see you back here," Detective Williams said.

"Okay, I'll be here waiting." The detectives walked out of the police station and got into their car. A couple of police vehicles drove behind them on their way to Calvin Bruno's loft.

“Why did you ask Emily that? I thought we were done asking her questions?” Detective Stevenson asked Detective Williams defensively once they were in the car.

“We’re never done asking questions, Stevie. We’re detectives, that's what we do.”

“But it’s the way you asked it. You asked the question like you were interrogating her, like she committed the crime. So what, now you don’t trust her?”

“If I’m being completely honest, no.”

“How can you not trust her? She’s the 18-year-old foster kid whose sister just died, remember?”

“I realize all of that, Stevie, but I just feel like there are some things she’s not telling us. She didn’t immediately tell us where her mother was, she doesn’t want to go back and see her foster mother, Ms. Baker. She didn’t explain the car situation until I asked her. Someone on the other end of Andrea’s phone keeps texting her. She knows all of this information, told us all of this stuff, but failed to mention Calvin Bruno grabbing Andrea, pushing her up against the wall, and Andrea being afraid of him.”

"Williams, her sister just died, okay? She forgot to share all of those details. It hasn't been that long since we showed her Andrea's dead body."

"I get that. I get all that, but she just seems a bit off to me. How she wanted to come to your place. She doesn't know you. Why did she want to stay with you? Why did Emily never file a missing person's report when Andrea was gone for that long. Now she wants to be a part of this case?"

"Correction, I invited her to my place. And she received text messages from Andrea's phone, so she thought everything was fine. What are you saying, Williams? The girl killed her sister?"

"I'm just saying we can't count anybody out. And you be careful — you don't know this girl, Stevie, and you have her at your home. This girl and her sister have been through a lot, and as we start opening Andrea's box, more and more deadly things are starting to come out."

"Well, I'm still looking for hope in that box."

"We're here." Detective Williams parked in front of Calvin Bruno's condo building. Detective Stevenson jumped out of the car aggressively, slammed the door, and walked into the condo building.

"Good morning. I'm Detective Stevenson, and this is Detective Williams. We have a warrant for Calvin Bruno's arrest. Can you tell us his apartment number?" Detective Stevenson said as she showed the security guard sitting at the front desk the arrest warrant and her badge.

"Fourth floor, apartment 4C," the security guard responded.

"Thank you. Williams and I will take the elevator, you guys take the stairs," Detective Stevenson ordered the other police officers who were with them. She and Detective Williams walked into the elevator and pressed the number four.

"I just don't understand why you're so upset about this. You don't think Emily seems a bit off? You don't feel like she's keeping information from us?"

"No, I don't feel like she's off. I feel like she's shaken up. The girl just found out her sister was murdered, Williams. And I don't think she's keeping things from us. She's 18, she's scared, she's confused, and she just lost the one person who cared about her. She told me today that Andrea's friends Veronica and Riley texted her today. If we don't get a confession soon, we can talk to her friends. Maybe they can tell us something."

"Alright Stevie, if you say so." Both detectives exited the elevator and walked to apartment 4C.

Knock. Knock. Knock.

"This is Detective Williams and Detective Stevenson. We have a warrant for the arrest of Calvin Bruno." No one answered the door. Detective Williams took his gun off his hip and so did Detective Stevenson. Detective Williams was about to have one of the other police officers kick in the door, when a young lady wearing a robe opened the door. The detectives put their guns down.

"Hello ma'am, we're looking for Calvin Bruno. We have a warrant for his arrest," Detective Stevenson said as she walked into the apartment holding the warrant. "Are you Lily Bostitch?"

"Yes, I am. Calvin is in the shower. What is all of this about? Why are you arresting him?" Lily asked, hysterical.

"Because, ma'am, Calvin is a suspect in the murder of Andrea Kane," Detective Williams explained.

"And who is Andrea Kane? How is my Calvin connected to her?"

"Andrea Kane and Calvin Bruno were in an intimate relationship. On the day that she died, she was going to see him. Based on our evidence, he is the last known person who saw her before she died. He was going on a trip to a conference in D.C., and he allegedly asked her to go with him," Detective Stevenson said.

"Wait, that trip to D.C., that was two weeks ago. And I couldn't go with him because I was out of town on a business trip. Is Andrea Kane the girl who I saw him with at the hotel?"

"We believe so," Detective Williams said.

"Excuse me, but before you arrest him, can I kill him?" Lily asked.

"No ma'am, you cannot do that. But you can come down to the police station with us. Maybe you can tell us what you know about him and Andrea's relationship?" Detective Stevenson suggested.

"Oh, Detective, I would gladly do so. Let me go get dressed." Lily Bostitch was about to head upstairs to her and Calvin's bedroom. Before she could get to the stairs, Calvin exited the bathroom in nothing but a towel, whistling. For a second, he didn't notice the detectives.

"Hey baby, do you want to try the food at that new restaurant up the street? I'm dying to…" Calvin finally looked up and saw Lily, the detectives, and four officers standing in his apartment. "Lily, what did you do?" Calvin asked. Lily grabbed a mug that was sitting on the counter filled with coffee that said “World’s Best Fiance” on it. She threw the mug at Calvin but he ducked down before it could hit him. The mug hit the wall instead and broke. “What’s the matter with you?”

“I don’t know, why don’t you ask Andrea Kane?” Lily said, sarcastically. After she asked this she held a knife in her hand that had been sitting on the counter next to her bagel that she had prepared for breakfast. The police officers pulled out their guns and told her to put the knife down.

“Whoa, put your guns down. Ma’am, we need you to put the knife down this instant. Go upstairs and get dressed,” Detective Williams said to the police officers and Lily.

“You’re lucky the police are here.” Lily set the knife down on the counter and walked upstairs to get dressed in the bathroom at the top of the loft, loudly saying slanderous things against Calvin.

“Calvin Bruno, we have a warrant for your arrest for the murder of Andrea Kane,” Detective Stevenson said as she held up the warrant. For a minute, Calvin just stood there.

“Andrea is dead?” he finally asked.

“Yes, and we have a warrant for your arrest,” Detective Stevenson responded.

“I didn’t kill Andrea. I want my lawyer,” Calvin responded, holding the towel that was wrapped around him.

“And he will be contacted at the police station while you’re sitting in an interrogation room.” Detective Williams beckoned a couple of officers to place handcuffs on Calvin.

“Can I at least get some clothes to put on?” Calvin asked, angrily.

“Of course,” Detective Stevenson said. “Oh, Lily?”

“Yes, Detective?” Lily came out of the bathroom wearing jeans and a bra and pulling her shirt over her head.

“Can you please bring something down for Calvin to wear on his way to the police station?”

“Oh, gladly, I know just the thing,” Lily walked into the closet and Calvin put his head down. “Does this work, Detective?” Lily asked as she held up a grandmother’s muumuu.

“Lily, please,” Calvin said.

“NO, CALVIN, YOU DON’T GET TO SAY ANYTHING,” Lily yelled as she walked downstairs to give the detectives the muumuu.

"I'll be waiting in my car, Detectives, or would you like for me to ride with you all?"

"You can ride with us, Ms. Bostitch," Detective Williams said. "You, sir, you can go ahead and put this on. There isn't a window in that bathroom, is there?"

"No sir," Lily responded as Calvin walked back to the bathroom to put on the muumuu.

"Ma'am why do you have a muumuu anyway?" Detective Stevenson asked.

"It belonged to my late grandmother. Don't worry, I'll get it back. I'll bring him a change of clothes to the station. I just want him to leave in that," Lily responded as Calvin walked out of the bathroom in the muumuu. The police officers began to handcuff him and escort him and Lily to the elevators in the hallway.

"So you took her to D.C. with you, huh, after you lied to me and told me that you were done with her?" Lily said while they were in the hallway waiting for the elevator, kicking Calvin in the calves.

"Ma'am, please, no violence," Detective Williams said.

"I hope you rot in prison," Lily said to Calvin since she couldn't get physical with him.

“I didn’t kill her, I didn’t kill anyone,” Calvin said defending himself.

“Well, none of this would be happening if you had left her alone and not invited her to D.C. with you,” Lily said as Calvin and three officers entered one elevator. The detectives decided it would be better to separate Calvin and Lily. They entered the other elevator with Lily and one other police officer. The drive back to the police station was filled with Lily complaining about her relationship with Calvin. The detectives regretted telling her that she could ride with them. The entire 15 minute drive was filled with Lily cursing, slandering Calvin, and saying that all men were scum. They finally arrived at the police station and placed Lily in one interrogation room and Calvin in the other, just as they had done with the Wrights. The detectives looked for Emily to tell her the good news.

“Alright Emily, we have Calvin Bruno, and Lily agreed to come in for questioning too,” Detective Stevenson said after Emily ran up to her. Detective Williams just looked at Emily; he was still feeling skeptical and didn’t understand why Detective Stevenson wasn’t.

“That’s great. Do you want me to text my sister’s phone while you’re interrogating them?” Emily asked.

"Sure. Now like I said, don't get your hopes up. This could be a dead end as well. I also want to talk to Veronica and Riley. Maybe Andrea mentioned something to them that could be useful or that you didn't remember," Detective Stevenson said.

"Okay, I'll text or call them tonight."

"Great, go ahead and sit behind the glass with the chief. We'll interrogate Calvin first," Detective Stevenson said.

"You sure you don't want to interrogate Lily first? She's not in police custody, so she could leave at any moment if she grows impatient," Detective Williams asked.

"You know what Williams, you're right. We'll start with Lily first," Detective Stevenson said.

"I may be right about other things as well," Detective Williams said under his breath. Detective Stevenson heard him and just rolled her eyes at him. She knew exactly what he meant by that, but Emily didn't hear him.

"What are you two waiting for?" the chief asked. "Let's go."

"Chief, we're going to interrogate Lily first. We don't have a warrant for her arrest, but she agreed to questioning. We don't want her to grow impatient or leave because something she says could be useful," Detective Stevenson said.

"Yeah, and Calvin wants his lawyer present during his interrogation," Detective Williams said.

"Okay, well let's talk to Lily first," the chief said as Detectives Williams and Stevenson walked into the interrogation room where Lily was sitting. Judging by her demeanor, Lily wasn't too happy to learn about Andrea and Calvin's recent rendezvous together.

"Men are such liars. After telling me that they weren't together anymore, he asks her to go to D.C. with him. How could he? Because I'm out of town for work, he decides to take the opportunity to talk to her again?"

"Lily, we have a statement from someone very close to Andrea that Calvin and Andrea never really stopped seeing each other," Detective Stevenson said.

"Wait, so you mean to tell me that he's been seeing her all this time? He's been lying to me the whole time?" Lily asked hysterically as her voice became louder and louder.

"I'm afraid so. Lily, were you aware of the nature of Calvin and Andrea Kane's relationship?" Detective Stevenson asked.

"Yeah, I'm guessing she was his side chick. You know, the other woman." Lily asserted.

"No, not exactly," Detective Stevenson started to say as she and Detective Williams sat down across from Lily.

"Well, Detective, what was it exactly?" Lily asked.

"Andrea Kane was a 20-year-old young woman who was a sugar baby. She had three sugar daddies, and Calvin was one of them," Detective Stevenson said as Lily just sat there in shock.

"Wait, what? So Calvin would pay her to be with him?" Lily finally asked.

"Basically. That's what a sugar daddy does. He would pay her to go on trips with him. He bought her different items of clothing, took her to nice hotels, things like that," Detective Williams said.

"Wow! I thought this was just another girl he was dating. I mean, when I saw them at the hotel together I got so jealous because she was gorgeous. Calvin likes younger women. I mean, you see, there is a huge age difference between us. He's 56 and I'm 31. I could tell when I saw her, and I only saw her that one time at the hotel, that she was younger. I freaked out. Calvin was a serial dater before we became serious. I thought he was done with that, but I guess not. He's a handsome doctor, and a lot of young women are attracted to him because of his looks and his career. I thought she was just another one of those girls, not a sugar baby."

"So when exactly did you see them at the hotel together?" Detective Stevenson asked.

"It was this past summer, I went out of town on a business trip. I came back a day early and wanted to surprise Calvin. On my way to our loft, I drove past a hotel. Calvin and… Andrea were walking into the hotel. I guessed they had been there for some time because they didn't have any bags with them. But I could tell it was them because of Calvin's clothes and the way he walks, and Calvin is 6'5, so you can't miss him. I immediately called him, and of course he lied. I'm guessing he put Andrea up in their hotel room. He came downstairs to talk to me. He got in my car and told me that things between him and her weren't serious. That he was going to stop talking to her because he didn't want to lose me. I hit him a few times and told him to get out of my car. I drove back to my apartment. I was upset with him, so I didn't answer the phone for a couple months. He kept calling, sending me gifts and flowers, and eventually we talked and made up. This past Christmas, he proposed, and we've been engaged ever since."

"It's a very nice ring," Detective Stevenson said.

"Yes, it is. Calvin is a wonderful man, just a huge liar and a cheat. He may be a liar and cheat, but I don't think he killed this girl. Especially if he took her to D.C. with him and was paying her to be with him. It seems to me that he wanted her to be in his life. It seems like I wasn't enough," Lily said looking down at her engagement ring, sadly.

"Lily, have you ever known Calvin to be violent?" Detective Williams asked to kill the awkward silence after Lily's last remark.

"No, not at all, why?" Lily answered.

"We have evidence that says that Calvin grabbed Andrea and pushed her up against a wall in their hotel room. He may not have seriously hurt her, but at that moment, she was afraid of him. After that, he left to talk to you, I'm guessing in the car, as you explained. He then went back upstairs with Andrea and we don't know much about what happened after that. We'll get his statement after we talk with you," Detective Williams said.

"No, he's never been violent with me, but I don't know if he was with her or not. Calvin didn't tell me much about her. He told me it wasn't serious. He pretended that he wasn't seeing her anymore when, as you say, he was seeing her the whole time. I mean, this man proposed to me on Christmas, and then I went out of town on business in late January, and he asked her to go to D.C. with him. I can't believe him," Lily responded angrily.

"So Lily, you've never met Andrea? Do you know who Nicholas Wright is?" Detective Stevenson asked.

"No, I never met her. To me it seems like Calvin was living a double life, so I'm sure he didn't want me to meet her. And no, I don't know anything about someone named Nicholas Wright. Who is that?"

"Never mind. Thank you, Lily, for your cooperation. We have no further questions. If you want you can leave," Detective Williams said.

"No problem, I hope I helped." Lily stood up to leave the interrogation room. "I'm going to go home. I'm going to move all of my things out of Calvin's loft and move back to my apartment. Can you give this to him? I'm done with him." Lily took off her engagement ring and set it on the table in the interrogation room before she left.

"We'll be sure to tell him," Detective Williams said. "You take care of yourself Ms. Bostitch."

"Thank you. I hope you find this girl's killer, she didn't deserve this." Lily left the interrogation room. The detectives went to the room on the other side of the interrogation window where the chief and Emily were standing.

"Bruno's lawyer is here, he's sitting in the interrogation room with him. This could go south, are you both ready for this?" The chief asked.

"Yeah, we're ready, Chief. It's not like we haven't done this before," Detective Stevenson said. "Emily, are you ready?"

"Yeah, also I texted the number while you were in with Lily. I just asked the person if everything was okay and if they're enjoying their time with Calvin. They said they were fine and they were enjoying their time."

"And we tried seeing where the phone's location was; it was in the West Loop. We looked at the camera footage, but we didn't see anyone with a matching coat, boots, or anything."

"Okay, so the person who has the phone isn't Lily or Calvin," Detective Williams added. "Alright Stevie, let's go in." Detective Williams and Detective Stevenson walked into the interrogation room where Calvin Bruno was sitting with his lawyer.

“Hi, I’m attorney Roger Hunt. I’m here to represent Calvin Bruno. I’ve already explained to him that anything he says can and will be used against him in a court of law. Mr. Bruno can speak for himself at any time, but I have advised him to speak as little as possible. He has told me why he’s under arrest, but he has informed me that he didn’t kill the young lady whose body you’ve found.”

“Hello Mr. Hunt, I’m Detective Stevenson, and this is Detective Williams. We’re the detectives in charge of Andrea Kane’s case. We understand that Calvin Bruno had an intimate relationship with Andrea Kane. On the day Andrea Kane died, she was on her way to see him. We were told by someone close to Andrea that she was supposed to go to D.C. with Calvin where he was going to speak at a conference.”

“Well my client doesn’t want to respond…” Attorney Hunt started to say before Calvin interjected.

“No, I want to speak. I want to clear my name, and I want to do that much for Andrea. She was an amazing woman and I want to help them with finding her murderer.”

“You do realize that this can be detrimental to you?” Attorney Hunt asked Calvin.

"Well, I have an alibi, and I think I can clear this whole thing up if I just tell them the truth."

"Alright then, Mr. Bruno, whenever…" Detective Stevenson began before Calvin interrupted her to correct her.

"Dr. Bruno, it's Dr. Bruno to you."

"Okay, Dr. Bruno. Whenever you're ready to give us your statement, we're ready to hear it." Detective Stevenson sat down and stared at Calvin to show that she wasn't intimidated by his position or interruption.

"Okay, where do you want me to begin?" Calvin asked with his hands cuffed on the table and his head down.

"Well you can start by explaining to us what a 56-year-old man was doing with a 20-year-old sugar baby. You can explain how you met Andrea Kane. From what we know from Lily and other sources, you're quite popular with young women because of your looks, your status, and your pockets. So why Andrea Kane?" Detective Williams asked as he leaned forward to look into Calvin's eyes.

"Well if you must know, yes, a lot of younger women are attracted to me. I've had serious relationships and been engaged many times to different women, but it always ends because of me being unfaithful. I can't help it, I haven't been faithful in any relationship I've ever been in. I've always been able to have a slew of women. I realize that women are attracted to my looks, my status, and my pockets, as you said, and I don't push them away if they want to be with me. Younger women and older women are attracted to me, but I usually date younger women."

"Why is that?" Detective Stevenson said.

"Why not? Younger women are more fun, less serious, and they're usually from have a lower income bracket than me so I can call the shots in the relationship. Older women usually want to be married, something I know I don't want for a long time. Older women usually have their own money and want to call the shots in the relationship. They aren't appreciative of me, what I give them, and what I have. I don't feel needed, wanted, or loved by them. I just feel like an object in their lives."

"Sort of like what you do with the younger women? You know, they're just objects in your life," Detective Stevenson asked.

"I'm a psychologist, Detective. I understand that the position I want women to be in when they're in a relationship with me, is not the position I want to be in. I'm an alpha male who likes damsels in need of me, my money, and my time." Calvin Bruno smirked.

"Well Lily Bostitch doesn't seem like that kind of woman," Detective Williams said.

"She's not, and that's what attracted me to her. Lily was young and beautiful, but she had her own money and her own mind. I hadn't met a girl like her. Our relationship was a tug of war, but we understood each other, we had fun together, it was nice having a woman who knows something about money, and who is cultured and well-traveled. She introduced me to things — it wasn't just me introducing her to things."

"So then why did you cheat on her?" Detective Stevenson said.

"Like I said, as much as I love Lily, I've never been faithful in a relationship. Lily isn't the first woman that I've proposed to. There have been eight women in my life that I've proposed to. I usually just propose to keep them around. I guess part of my issue is I want to be the one to call the shots, and I also want to be the one to say if we're breaking up or not."

"So you propose to women just to keep them around, because they're about to leave you because you're cheating on them? Only to turn around and break up with them because you want to call the shots? I just want to make sure I have this correct," Detective Stevenson asked.

"Yes, that's exactly it. So I proposed to Lily because she broke up with me because she saw Andrea and I going into the hotel. It worked like a charm, always does." Calvin Bruno smiled.

"That's very deceitful and controlling of you, Dr. Bruno," Detective Stevenson asserted.

"Yes, but the women I've had in my life have made it so easy. Of course I've had a few stalkers, harassers, and even a fatal attraction moment, but it's all worth it for the time I spend with the women." Calvin Bruno sat back in his chair confidently.

"You're digging yourself a very deep hole here," Attorney Hunt said, looking at Calvin displeased.

"Well it's my story to tell, so I'm telling it," Calvin Bruno responded in anger.

"So tell us the story of how you met Andrea Kane," Detective Williams prompted.

"I met Andrea at a party. It was more like a soiree, and she was there with some other guy."

"Was this other guy Nicholas Wright?" Detective Williams asked.

"I don't know who he was. He was just some short, plump guy with a receding hairline and male pattern baldness. Andrea looked too good to be with him, and I felt that she would look better on my arm. Things had just started with Lily at this time, but I didn't ask her to come with me just in case I did meet another woman at this soiree."

"So what kind of soiree was this?" Detective Stevenson asked.

"It was an auction for a non-profit organization. They were trying to raise money to put into some low-income neighborhood in Chicago. I think it was for family housing, a community center, something like that. I just donated $30,000 to the cause by buying a painting that night. Anyway, the soiree was around this time last year. I saw Andrea standing there. She had brunette hair that draped across her tan skin. Her hair was slightly curled. She was wearing a red dress and had red lips. Her dress hugged her in all the right places and she just took my breath away. So I had to go over to where she was and talk to her. She was just standing next to a table, looking beautiful yet out of place. The guy she was with was working the room, I guess doing business. He wasn't paying her much attention. I guess he wanted her to walk in with him, and everyone saw them together so that was enough for him. Everyone in these circles knew that I would flirt with their women, and their women would flirt with me. Men at these things would keep their women close. I guess either this guy didn't know about my behavior, or he didn't care."

"Okay, proceed Dr. Bruno," Detective Williams said.

"When I saw an opportunity, I walked up to Andrea as she was standing there, and I said, 'You look lonely, where is your date?' She pointed in his direction, and I told her that if she were my date I would never leave her side. She smiled that gorgeous smile of hers. We talked for a bit, flirting here and there. I told her my name and what I did. She seemed interested after that. She slipped me her card before the guy she was with called her to come over and stand next to him. I watched her walk away, and once she stood next to him I looked at her card. It said her name, her number, and on the back it said 'professional sugar baby.' I didn't know exactly what that meant, so I googled it on my phone. I realized that it meant she was looking for a sugar daddy. I thought that maybe the guy she came to the soiree with was her sugar daddy already, but if she gave me her card, maybe she could use another one. So I called her."

"So you were all for the sugar baby thing, even if you had to share her?" Detective Williams asked.

"Yeah, I was fine with it. I thought this would be a great opportunity for her and I. She wanted someone with money to support her, and I just wanted a young lady to have fun with and spend time with. It wouldn't be anything serious, which I liked. I asked her how this whole thing worked and told her that I'd never had a professional sugar baby before. She told me that she would meet me and go places with me. We would spend time together, and we could do whatever I wanted. In return, I just had to pay her, give her things, stuff like that. I had never done this before, so I wanted to try it out. I took her out to dinner at a nice hotel; we spent the night together, had a wonderful time, and she and I had been together ever since."

"Did she know you were dating Lily?" Detective Williams asked.

"No, not until around April. She looked at one of my social media pages and saw Lily on there. One day, while we were in Dubai together, she asked me if Lily was my girlfriend. I usually lie to women when they ask me this question, but I didn't lie to Andrea. She wasn't uptight or upset, and she didn't ask me in an interrogative way. She just seemed to be asking me a question. So I told her the truth that

Lily was my girlfriend. She told me that Lily was pretty and that I was a lucky guy. Then she asked me if Lily knew about her, and I told her Lily didn't. She asked me if this would interfere with our time together, and she worried that I wouldn't have time for her. I told her that it wouldn't interfere with anything and that I would make time."

"When exactly did Lily find out about Andrea?" Detective Stevenson asked.

"When we came back from Dubai, Lily was suspicious. She kept asking who I spent time with in Dubai, so I told her that I spent time with some friends there. She asked me what happened, and I told her that what happens in Dubai stays in Dubai. I took a shower after this, left my phone out and Andrea texted me. Lily didn't know the password to my phone, but the text messages popped up on my screen, and she could see Andrea's text message. Andrea texted me to tell me she had a great time in Dubai, and she couldn't wait until we saw each other again."

"Was Andrea's name attached to the text? You know, was her contact name Andrea in your phone?" Detective Stevenson asked.

"No, in my phone, her name was 'red dress.' That's what she was wearing when I saw her that blew my mind. So I had to put a name in that I would remember her by. I date a lot of women as you all know, so I have to give them names that help me remember them. Curvy blonde, blue-eyed brunette, girl with nice bum at party, girl with double D's from the beach, things like that. Lily was upset, so I told her that this was a girl I was dating before I met her. She didn't want to speak to me again, so we broke up for a few weeks. I told Andrea about it and I gave her a separate number for another phone I had. That way Lily wouldn't ever know that we were still seeing each other. Andrea agreed to it and apologized for texting me since Lily saw it. She was sweet like that. I told her that it wasn't her fault.

Lily and I made up and we were good for some time. I would see Andrea here and there, send her money when I could. In August, Lily had to go on a business trip for work. She works for Google and would be gone for two and half weeks. She told me she would be gone for three weeks. I decided to call Andrea to see if she wanted to spend some time together. We went to Mauritius for two weeks because she told me she wanted to get away with me for a little bit before Lily returned. She knew that once Lily returned, she wouldn't see me for a while. I told her that I knew just the place. We came back to Chicago after those two weeks and stayed at a hotel downtown, and Lily saw us coming into the hotel after having brunch at a restaurant. She saw Andrea, and she flipped out. She didn't know her name, and she asked if that was the girl I was in Dubai with. I told her it was."

"Was this the time that you grabbed Andrea and pushed her up against the wall?" Detective Stevenson asked, and Calvin looked surprised for a minute.

"Is that a crime, Detective?" Calvin grinned and asked.

"No it isn't, but you're a suspect in this case mainly because of that incident. Andrea claimed to a source that she was afraid of you after this," Detective Stevenson responded.

Calvin took a big sigh and said, "Andrea was trying to leave and I didn't want her to go. She tried leaving after she realized that Lily saw us and called me. She didn't want Lily to be upset and she didn't want Lily and I to break up. I grabbed her arm so she wouldn't leave and she told me to let her go. That's when I pulled her, held on to her arms, and put her against the wall. She did look startled when I did this. I yelled at her a bit and told her to wait here and that I would handle everything," Calvin paused to look into the detectives' eyes and then continued. "I'm not a violent man at all. I'm a lover not a fighter. I just didn't want Andrea to go. After Lily broke up with me and left, I went back upstairs with Andrea. I could tell she was upset and scared. I told her that I was sorry and that I would never do anything to hurt her."

"You're also a suspect because you were the last person that Andrea was supposed to see the day she died. Tell us what happened on January 28th when you all went out for breakfast?" Detective Williams said.

"I hadn't seen Andrea for a couple months, so I told her that I wanted to see her. Lily was out of town for a business trip, and I was going to surprise Andrea with a trip to D.C. I told her I wanted to meet for breakfast. She told me she would meet me at the place if I just let her know where it was. We had breakfast together and I invited her to come to D.C. with me. At first she wasn't too excited about it; she didn't pack a suitcase or anything. I told her not to worry and that we would get her some clothes and go shopping once we got to D.C. We took an Uber to the airport. Our flight left at 12:00 in the afternoon, so we needed to be there by 10:00. Andrea rode all the way to the airport with me and then told me that she didn't want to come. She said she didn't feel right leaving her sister like that without really telling her she was leaving. So I kissed her goodbye and that was the last time I saw her."

"So you boarded the plane and left her at the airport?" Detective Stevenson asked.

"Yeah, since we already had an Uber, she just hopped back in. I told her to text me so that I could pay the person once she got back home."

"Did she ever text you?" Detective Williams asked.

"No she didn't so I figured she paid for it herself."

"Dr. Bruno, when was the last time you talked to Andrea Kane?" Detective Williams asked.

"Um…February 1st, I texted her and told her I was back in town if she wanted to meet up. She told me she did, and then when I asked her when, she never responded. I guess she was gone by then."

"Yeah, that's what her autopsy revealed," Detective Williams said.

"So the person that killed her may have her phone?" Calvin Bruno asked confused.

"That's what we're thinking," Detective Stevenson said.

"Okay, Dr. Bruno, we're going to get a copy of your phone records to check in with your alibis. Make sure you were at that conference and that Andrea Kane did leave the airport once you boarded."

"Fine, I'll just wait until you hear everything and let me go. I'll have to go home and make up with Lily."

"Oh yeah, we almost forgot. Lily wanted us to give you this," Detective Stevenson said, as she placed Lily's engagement ring on the table. "She wanted us to tell you that she's done with you as well."

Detective Stevenson and Detective Williams walked out of the interrogation room as Calvin Bruno sat looking at the engagement ring he gave to Lily. In his mind, he knew that it was truly over because she gave the ring back. He sat there while his lawyer told him how stupid he was for giving the detectives all of this information, but he didn't care. He knew that they would check his alibis and find out that he had nothing to do with Andrea's death. The detectives walked behind the window to talk with the chief and Emily.

"I already put some of the guys on the alibis. They'll check in about the conference in D.C., and someone is going to head over to the airport to see the camera footage," the chief said.

"Great, Chief, but we can head over to the airport now to ask for the camera footage. We have to wait for Calvin's alibis to see if he actually went to the conference," Detective Williams assured the chief.

"Yeah, we can head to the airport now. See the camera footage and ask if Calvin Bruno boarded the plane while we're there," Detective Stevenson added.

"Okay, we'll keep Calvin here, and Emily, you can stay here as well. Even if his alibi checks out, we'll still hold him until you view that camera footage to see that he did board that plane and that she left in the Uber. I'll also check to see if Lily Bostitch was actually out of town, or if she was trying to trap Calvin in a lie," the chief responded.

"Emily, will you be okay?" Detective Stevenson asked Emily.

"Yeah, I'll be fine," Emily responded with her head hanging down. She'd started feeling defeated. Here they were, still with no true arrest for her sister's murder. They were running out of sugar daddies, and Albert Little and his wife were the least likely to be Andrea's killer.

"Hey, don't worry. We'll figure this out," Detective Stevenson said, placing her hand on Emily's shoulder. She noticed that Emily looked defeated.

"Okay." Emily responded. The detectives got into their car to ride to the airport. While they were on their way, Detective Williams and Detective Stevenson began talking about the situation with Calvin and Lily.

"So what do you think about these two?" Detective Williams asked.

"I don't know, it seems sketchy. Lily was out of town, but she may not have been. The Wrights seemed like the main suspects, but they were only connected to the murder because of the construction site and Nicholas being Andrea's sugar daddy. Then Calvin leaves her at the airport, so she never went to D.C. with him. But she never came home either. Amber Wright has a boyfriend and wouldn't be jealous of Andrea, and Nicholas wasn't focused on being with Andrea. I'm just confused, and I'm starting to feel like we're hitting a wall. Nothing's making any sense. Andrea's dead body was found at Nicholas's construction site and Calvin was the last person that she was with, but now both of them seem to be clean."

"Well, we still have Albert Little and his wife."

"Yeah, but what if we can't get a warrant for his arrest? He threatened Andrea, but his 'or else' could've meant anything."

"Yeah, but maybe we can still use that. Look, we may not be able to get Samantha Little in for questioning. We don't have much evidence for her, but maybe she'd be willing to come if she knows anything about Andrea. And we still have the text messages to Emily."

"Yeah, I guess you're right."

"Don't throw in the towel just yet, Stevie, we'll figure this out. Besides, I'm still not counting Emily out."

"Are you still on that?" Detective Stevenson was disgusted.

"Yes, I feel like there is still something she's not telling us. It doesn't have to be anything big. It could be a fight she and Andrea had — maybe some things were said that she regrets."

"I can say that she can be a bit distant, but we did just meet her."

"Maybe you should grill her a bit when you talk to her today. You know, see if she tells you anything."

"I'll do it, just to prove you wrong." Detective Williams parked the car to go into the airport. The detectives walked over to the receptionist desk to figure out who they could speak with about the camera footage.

"Walk with me, Detectives," the receptionist said as she led them to the camera room. "This is our camera room, and this is Mr. Thompson. He'll tell you everything."

"Detectives, what do you need?" Mr. Thompson asked.

"We need you to go to the date of January 28th at around 10:00 am. There should have been passengers coming in. One is the suspect in a murder and one is the murdered, we need to see them both," Detective Williams said.

"Okay, let me get the footage and then I'll play it for you." Mr. Thompson played the footage from January 28th and fast forwarded to 10:00 am.

"There, stop right there, and slow that down," Detective Stevenson said as she saw the images of Calvin and Andrea. In the video, you could see Calvin talking to Andrea, holding her hand. Then he gave her a kiss and went inside the airport as she got back in the car. "Mr. Thompson, how do we find out if that man got on his flight?"

"Go back to the receptionist desk and ask them, they should be able to tell you." The detectives headed back to the receptionist desk.

"Hi, would you be able to look back to January 28th and see if a man by the name Calvin Bruno boarded his flight to D.C. at 12:00 pm?" Detective Williams asked the receptionist.

"Yes, let me check that for you," the receptionist said. "Okay, yes, I see a Dr. Calvin Bruno boarded a flight to D.C. He originally paid for two tickets, but he canceled the second ticket while here and wanted to know if he could get his money back."

"Thank you, that's all we needed today," Detective Stevenson said as she and Detective Williams exited the airport. "Alright, we have to tell the chief about the camera footage and the boarded flight."

"So, now we have to try to get a warrant for Albert Little. Or do you think he'd be willing to come in for interrogation?" Detective Williams asked.

"I don't know, but we can try to get the warrant. If we can't get the warrant, then we can try asking him about his relationship with Andrea. Maybe we can go to one of his classes at the University of Illinois in Chicago, see if he'd be willing to talk?"

The detectives walked back into the police station, defeated. Calvin Bruno could go free based on the information that they got from the airport. Once they walked back in, the chief called both detectives into his office.

"What's the matter, Chief?" Detective Stevenson asked as she walked into the chief's office. She wondered if Emily let it slip that she was staying with her.

"His alibi checks out. What did you find at the airport?" the chief asked.

"The video showed that Calvin did walk into the airport, and Andrea got back into the Uber. Calvin also canceled Andrea's ticket to D.C. He was there at 10:00 am, and at 12:00 pm, he was on his flight to D.C. So his story checks out," Detective Williams explained.

"So that means we really only have one suspect left in this case. Lily Bostitch's alibi checks out too, so she was out of town at the time. It seems that the sugar daddies and their wives and girlfriends aren't the murderers. There has to be someone else involved here. Now that we have video footage, it seems that after she left Calvin at the airport, somehow Andrea Kane came in contact with another person. That person killed her, got her phone, and texted Emily. So all those text messages about being in D.C., being at a basketball game, going to Florida with Nicholas, are all a lie," the chief said.

"So do you want us to leave Albert Little alone?" Detective Stevenson asked.

"I'm not saying that you can't bring him in. You can even bring his wife in, but I think we'll still hit a wall. I know you thought what Emily told you would be helpful, but it hasn't been. Now you all have to start doing real detective work. Get your boots to the ground □ stop depending on her information and ask more questions of more individuals and see what you can come up with. You all are better than this. Do the work, even if it's going to take more time and more effort. We'll try to get Albert Little in for interrogation tomorrow, but after that, do the work," the chief responded looking both detectives in the eyes to let them know how serious he was.

"Yes Chief," Detective Stevenson said.

"Alright, Calvin Bruno is off. Let the man go, and give him some real clothes. See if you can get Albert Little in tomorrow, and if you can't, go by his home or his job and try to talk to him about his relationship with Andrea Kane. If everything checks out with him, check in with Andrea's friends and do the work. You both are dismissed." The chief waved his hand so the detectives could leave his office.

"See what I mean? Nothing she's given us has helped us. We've been hitting dead ends because of her. It's something she's not telling us," Detective Williams said after he and Detective Stevenson left the chief's office.

"Okay, I'll talk to her. I'll tell her that we need more information or something, but you can't say that she hasn't been helpful. We interrogated these men because of Emily. And yes, their stories check out now, but before interrogation, they were prime suspects. You know that."

"Yes, they were prime suspects. But now they're not. Emily and this phone thing are dragging us down. Did you tell her to tell the person who has Andrea's phone that she knows that they're the killer?"

"No, I didn't."

"Well Stevie, you need to start. The chief calling us into his office means he's serious. You're already playing a dangerous game by having her at your house. Get it together. I'll let Calvin Bruno know he can go, so you find Emily and talk to her." Detective Williams walked away to get Calvin Bruno's clothes and let him go. Detective Stevenson went to look for Emily. She found her coming out of the bathroom.

"Hey, so what did you guys find?" Emily asked. Detective Stevenson didn't know exactly what to say to her. She thought strongly about what Detective Williams and the chief had said about Emily.

"Let's go back to my place so we can talk."

"That doesn't sound good," Emily said, frightened. As she said this, Calvin Bruno was walking towards the bathroom to change into his clothes. "Can we go? I don't want to see him."

"Emily, why?" Detective Stevenson asked.

"I don't want him to know I'm here. I don't want him to see me," Emily ran back into the women's bathroom, frantic and scared.

"Emily, Emily wait." Detective Stevenson ran in the bathroom after her. "Emily, what are you hiding? Why don't you want to see Calvin Bruno?"

"I just don't want to see him." Emily hid in one of the stalls.

"Emily, you have to tell me the truth. Why are you afraid of seeing Calvin Bruno? Did he do something to you?"

"No, that's not it." Emily sat in the stall with tears streaming down her face.

"Emily, you have to tell me the truth. The chief and Detective Williams are already skeptical of you."

"What do you mean they're skeptical of me?"

"Williams thinks you're hiding something from us, and the chief thinks you haven't shared any valuable information with us. Now you're running into bathrooms afraid to see Calvin Bruno. What is this about?" When Detective Stevenson asked this, Emily walked out of the bathroom stall. She stared at Detective Stevenson while tears were still running down her face. She was heartbroken to hear Detective Stevenson's brutal honesty, but it made her tell the truth.

"I didn't want to see Calvin Bruno because he was a guest speaker at my school for one of my psychology courses. He was the best speakers, psychologists, and doctors I had ever heard. When Andrea told me she was dating him, I definitely didn't approve. We had a big argument, and she got upset. We didn't talk for a couple of weeks. We only made up when she asked me to move in with her. I didn't want my sister to be a sugar baby to one of the professors that I looked at so highly. I loved what he had to say, his wit, his sense of humor, and the way he taught. I hung onto every word he said. Then I found out my big sister was his sugar baby."

"Emily, I am so sorry."

"I was hurt to find out he was such a creep. I was hurt to know that before my sister died, she had gone to see him. I was hurt to know that I had learned so much from a person that I looked at so highly, and he let me down. And so did my sister. I know I may have hidden this from you all, but it was only because it hurts too bad to admit it. I also didn't want you guys to think I was trying to get back at Calvin or something. But now that he's going home free, I guess it's okay for me to admit."

"Emily, I didn't know. I'm sorry for…"

"You know, you said Detective Williams thought I was hiding something and the chief felt that I didn't share any valuable information. What do you think? Do you feel how they feel?" Emily asked, but in the back of her mind she knew that Detective Stevenson did believe what they were saying.

"No, Emily, I feel that we wouldn't have interrogated this many suspects and gotten this far without you. And yes, you were hiding something, but I didn't think you were. I thought you were just in pain. What you were hiding also came from a place of pain. I understand." Emily stood in front of Detective Stevenson in the women's restroom, staring at her in disbelief.

"Can you take me to Mama Kim's house? I promised her I would see her today."

"Yeah. Yeah, I'll take you there now," Detective Stevenson said, shocked. She hoped that she hadn't upset Emily by telling her everything about the chief and Detective Williams. She hoped that Emily wouldn't do anything to harm herself or do something irrational. Detective Williams walked out of the bathroom to see if Calvin Bruno was gone, and she saw Detective Williams.

"Hey Williams, is Calvin gone?" Detective Stevenson asked.

"Yeah, why?" Detective Williams asked concerned.

"Nothing, I'll tell you later. Emily wants me to take her to Ms. Baker's house. Will you be here when I get back?"

"No, I'll be at home, but you can come by. I won't be asleep. What's wrong? Did something happen between you two?"

"I'll tell you when I stop by. Let me go get Emily so I can take her to Ms. Baker's house," Detective Stevenson walked back to the bathroom to go get Emily. When Detective Stevenson walked into the bathroom, Emily was just standing there crying and biting her nails.

"Emily, Calvin is gone. I can take you to Ms. Baker's house now." Emily exited the bathroom without saying a word to Detective Stevenson. They left the police station, got in Detective Stevenson's car, and drove to Ms. Kimberly Baker's house. On the way there, Emily still didn't say a word to Detective Stevenson. Once they got to Ms. Kimberly Baker's house, Emily finally gave her more information.

"I'm just going to stay here tonight on Mama Kim's couch. I'll meet you at the police station tomorrow morning before you go to interrogate Albert Little. Oh and here, this is the address where Veronica and Riley are. They said they're willing to talk and they may have some information that might help with the case." Emily texted Detective Stevenson the address.

"Okay, thank you. Emily, I'm so sorry about what I said…"

"I'll see you tomorrow. I have to go see how Mama Kim is doing." Emily exited the car and walked up to Ms. Kimberly Baker's porch to ring the doorbell. Ms. Kimberly Baker opened the door, gave Emily a long hug, waved at Detective Stevenson, and told Emily to come in. At that moment, Detective Stevenson knew she had upset Emily. She knew that she had doubted Emily just like Williams and the chief had. That it wasn't the words that hurt Emily so much, but it was that Detective Stevenson had believed those words too. She knew deep down she'd agreed with Williams and the chief, and she could tell that Emily had felt that agreement. Detective Stevenson drove to Detective Williams' house in anger, frustration, and sadness. Once she arrived at his home, it took her some time to exit the car, walk up to his house, and ring the doorbell. When Detective Williams finally opened the door, he could tell something was wrong.

"Stevie, come in. What's up?" Detective Williams said, holding the door wide open.

"She hates me now." Detective Stevenson walked into Detective Williams' house and sat on a bar stool at his kitchen island.

"Who? Emily?" Detective Williams grabbed two beers from the fridge for him and Detective Stevenson.

"Yeah."

"Why? She was like your little shadow this morning and all while we've been working on this case." The detectives stood next to the kitchen counter and drank their beers.

"Because while I was talking to Emily at the bathroom door, Calvin was about to walk up. She got so scared and ran into the women's bathroom. I was confused as to why she didn't want to see Calvin Bruno, so I freaked out and started interrogating her."

"What did you say to her?"

"Everything you and the chief said started getting inside my head. I started feeling like Emily was keeping something from us, from me. So I told her that you felt that she was holding something back and that the chief felt that she only led us to dead ends and hasn't helped much with this case."

"You told her that?" Detective Williams asked as he almost choked on his sip of beer.

"Yeah, I did. It slipped out, I didn't mean to. I was frantic, and I wanted to know why she didn't want to see Calvin Bruno," Detective Stevenson waved her hands around in frustration.

"Well, why didn't she want to see him?"

"Because, Calvin Bruno was a guest speaker at Emily's school. She really liked him, she looked at him highly. And she was upset to find out that Andrea was a sugar baby to a psychologist she looked at so highly. She and Andrea got into a big fight about it, but they made up later. It hurt Emily to know that Andrea and Calvin were together, and the way they were together. It also hurt her that the day her sister was killed, the last person she saw was Calvin. It hurt Emily to think that he may have killed her sister."

"Wow, so she was hiding something. That's deep, why didn't she tell us?"

"She didn't want us to think she was trying to get back at Calvin for dating her sister. I think it hurt her feelings when I told her what I told her. She asked me to take her to Ms. Baker's house to spend some time with her. I think she felt that deep down I agreed with you all. And what you all said did get inside my head a bit, and I did doubt her."

"Well I was right, that she was hiding something. But she was hiding it because of hurt. I mean I get it. Will she come back to the station tomorrow for Albert Little's interrogation?"

"She said she'll drive over in Andrea's car. I feel so stupid."

"I'm sorry. I feel like part of this is my fault for getting inside your head. I should've kept my thoughts to myself."

"No, you were just doing your job. Anyway, Emily gave me the address where Veronica and Riley are staying. She texted them back, and they told her that they may have some information that may be helpful in finding Andrea's murderer."

"That's great. We'll check them out after talking to Albert and Samantha." Detective Williams could tell Detective Stevenson was still upset.

"Hey Stevie, don't worry. I'm sure Emily will be fine, and you'll see her tomorrow morning."

"I don't know, Williams, I worry about that kid. I feel like I was the one thing that was keeping her from doing something stupid. Where are Cheryl and the boys?"

"Oh, she went to visit her mom, so they should be coming back home soon."

"Okay, I'm going to head home."

"Hey, if it'll make you feel better, why don't you go over to Ms. Baker's house and talk to Emily?" Detective Williams walked Detective Stevenson to the door.

"Yeah, maybe I will." Detective Stevenson entered her car and drove back to Ms. Kimberly Baker's house to see Emily again. She parked her car and rang the doorbell. Ms. Kimberly Baker answered the door.

"Hi Detective Stevenson, are you here to see Emily?"

"Yeah, I just wanted to make sure she was okay."

"Come in, she's eating in the kitchen." Detective Stevenson walked into the kitchen and saw Emily eating. Her back was turned to the detective, but she'd heard her come in.

"What are you doing back here? I told you I would come by the police station tomorrow," Emily said without turning around.

"I just wanted to make sure you were okay. I know I said some pretty harsh things at the police station out of fear and anger. I shouldn't have done that to you. You've been nothing but cooperative this entire time. You've given us so much information, and I shouldn't have doubted you. I shouldn't have let anyone persuade me to look at you differently. I'm sorry Emily."

"It's fine, you were just doing your job. I get it, I was hiding something from you all and I shouldn't have done that. It was just hard to admit. I'm sorry too. I still want to stay with Mama Kim tonight, though."

"That's fine. If you want me to come pick you up tomorrow, I can."

"No, I'll just drive Dre's car tomorrow. Don't worry, I'll be there in the morning. Afterwards we can go see Riley and Veronica and see what they know."

"You got it all planned out, huh, little detective?" Detective Stevenson smiled.

"I'm being mentored by the best, right?" Emily still didn't turn around to face Detective Stevenson, but she smiled too.

"Okay, I'll see you tomorrow," Detective Stevenson walked to the door. "Thank you Ms. Baker."

"Oh no, thank you, Detective. Emily told me all that you've done for her. It's because of you and Detective Williams that she had the courage to come tell me how everything is going. I'm going to try to plan a memorial for Andrea. We don't have enough money for a burial, funeral, all of that. I think we'll just cremate her," Ms. Kimberly Baker said as she and Detective Williams walked out the door.

"Is that what Emily wants?" Detective Stevenson asked.

"I don't know for sure, she didn't say anything when I told her." Ms. Kimberly Baker stood on the porch with Detective Stevenson.

"Okay, I'll ask her tomorrow. And if she wants a funeral and burial for her sister, I'll try to think of something. I'll see you later Ms. Baker."

"Okay, see you, Detective."

After their conversation, Detective Stevenson drove home. As she walked into her condo, she noticed what Emily was talking about. She noticed how disastrous her place looked. She decided to wash her dishes, do her laundry, organize her papers, and put her clothes away. Once she was done, she decided to go to a bar where some of the other police officers liked to go after work. She decided to put herself out there and have fun like Emily told her.

Chapter 6 - Albert & Samantha Little

Detective Stevenson woke up the next day, February 12th, and felt better than she ever had before due to her place being cleaned and organized. After taking a shower, she did something she didn't usually do in the morning. She made herself some coffee and cooked some scrambled eggs and toast. She looked over some paperwork and folded her laundry before heading to work. After drinking her coffee and eating her breakfast, she got a text from Emily.

On my way to the police station.

Great, on my way too. Emily responded.

Detective Stevenson left her papers on the table, but this time she organized them. She threw on her coat, her badge, and her gun, got in her car, and drove to the police station. She felt a sense of relief knowing Emily was on her way to the police station as well. When she finally arrived in front of the police station, she saw Emily sitting in her car. She exited her car and knocked on Emily's window.

Once Emily rolled down the window, Detective Stevenson asked her,

"Why are you still sitting in your car?"

"After what you told me yesterday, I didn't want to go in without you." Emily looked away from Detective Stevenson and held her head down.

"Yeah, I probably shouldn't have told you that. Listen, Williams does want to apologize to you. I told him about what happened with you and Calvin Bruno. Come on, we gotta get started." Emily got out of the car after Detective Stevenson said this. They walked into the police station together and sat down on a bench inside. "How are you going to feel when you have to stay here while we go to talk to Albert Little at his place?"

"I should be okay. I'll just sit in the back. I've been talking to Veronica and Riley, telling them about the case, so I'll probably tell them some more stuff. They're worried about me."

"Have they told you what they know yet?"

"No, they said you can come by their place, or they can come by the police station to give a statement if you want. They're fine with whatever."

"Why are they worried about you?"

"They knew how close Andrea and I were, and they were close to her too. They're worried that I won't have anyone now. They told me I can move in with them for as long as I want."

"Is that what you want?"

"I don't know. I don't know what I want yet. I just want justice to be served for my sister at this point. I don't think about what I'm going to eat, where I'm going to go, or what I'm going to wear."

"Yeah, I brought you some more clothes in case you needed to change. Do you need to shower?"

"I had some old clothes at Mama Kim's house. I hadn't changed my underwear in a couple of days, so I needed to stop by, shower, change my clothes, and spend some time with her. She loved Andrea too, and she deserves to know what's been going on with her case."

"How did she take everything? Did you tell her everything?"

"I did. I told her about Andrea's life as a sugar baby, her sugar daddies, their wives and girlfriends, and her murder's connection to them. I told her why Andrea didn't want to tell her everything. She was confused and she told me that she wished Andrea would've been honest with her. That she wasn't a judgemental person. Of course, she would've been scared for Andrea, but she wouldn't have pushed her to do anything she didn't want to do. She was sad, upset, and hurt that Andrea didn't know that before she died."

"I'm sorry that you had to do that, Emily."

"You know, I don't think Andrea felt that Mama Kim would've been judgemental or ashamed of her. I think deep down, Dre was ashamed of what she was doing. She was ashamed that this was the way she lived her life, the way she made her money, and that's why she didn't tell Mama Kim."

"Ms. Baker told me that she was going to have Andrea cremated and that you all would have a memorial for her. I asked her if that's what you wanted. She told me she didn't know for sure, so I wanted to ask you."

"I don't know, I haven't thought much about it. I guess I don't need to visit Andrea's grave. I can have her ashes. Or Mama Kim and I can share her ashes. A memorial would be fine, I guess."

"Well, let me know. If you want a funeral, I can help you all with that. If you want to have her cremated, I can help you all with that too." Both of them stood up and walked to Detective Williams' desk.

“Alright Williams, did you do your magic and get a warrant for Albert’s arrest?” Detective Stevenson asked.

“No, the Williams magic didn’t work this time. So we’ll have to see if Albert is at his house, if he’s teaching at the University of Illinois in Chicago, or if he’s actually performing surgery. I hope it’s not the latter,” Detective Williams responded.

“Alright, so that makes things a bit more complicated. What about the wife? Maybe we can talk to her first before we begin looking for him?” Detective Stevenson asked.

“Samantha Little lives with their daughter in Oak Park. Get this, the week prior to Andrea’s death, Samantha filed for divorce from Albert. So I guess they were separated all of that time like Emily said, and then she served Albert with papers.” Detective Williams said.

“So you’re thinking…”

“It’s a stretch, but with Emily’s statement about Albert wanting to get serious with Andrea, and threatening her if she didn’t break up with Nicholas and Calvin, it seems like a motive to want to hurt Andrea if she didn’t do it. Then to know that his wife filed for divorce meant that his life was falling apart; he’d lost one serious relationship and he wanted another one, but Andrea wasn’t for it. Not enough for a warrant, but enough to connect Albert Little to everything and question him."

"So we pay a visit to the wife in Oak Park, ask her a bit about Albert, the separation, the divorce. Then we go by his place, his job, or the university and question him. Have you talked to the chief about it?"

"Yeah, he said we can take a couple of the guys with us today." Detective Williams noticed Emily wasn't saying anything, and she was standing behind Detective Stevenson with her head down. "Stevie, can you give me and Emily a minute?"

"Yeah, I'll go get Flores and Brooks to come with us," Detective Stevenson said.

"Emily, could you sit here please?" Detective Williams asked. As Emily sat down timidly in a chair next to his desk, he said. "Look, I want to apologize for not trusting you and feeling like you had something to hide..."

"It wasn't all your fault. I was hiding something. I know that Detective Stevenson told you about Calvin Bruno. I should've told you all. You trusted me, and I should've trusted you. You were only trying to help, and I kept that from you all."

"Emily, did Calvin know that you and Andrea were sisters?" Detective Williams asked.

"No. He was a guest speaker at my college before they met. Andrea made sure she didn't tell him that I was her little sister."

"Do you think he made the connection because of your last name?"

"I don't know, I don't think so. He never mentioned anything to Dre. Kane is a popular last name. And I don't think Andrea told him my name was Emily. She just told her sugar daddies she had a little sister in college. Calvin may have realized that I was the little sister, but he may not have."

Ding. Ding.

"Hold on, that's a text message. It might be Veronica, or Riley, or Mama Kim." Emily pulled her phone from her pocket. She stared at her phone in disbelief and shock.

"Emily, what's wrong?" Detective Williams asked her.

"It's Andrea's number." Emily responded.

"What does it say?" Emily turned the phone around so Detective Williams could see. He read the text message.

I know you know. Sent from Andrea's phone at 9:05 am.

"Okay, this could be because of the chief's media statement. Or it could be from one of the suspects. We don't know, so don't freak out. We know whoever has your sister's phone is your sister's murderer."

"What do I say? Should I not resp…" Emily started to say as Detective Stevenson walked up.

"Hey, did you two make up? Williams, you ready to go?" Detective Stevenson noticed Emily and Detective Williams' faces. "You two look like you've seen a ghost."

"The murderer just texted me from Andrea's phone. They said, 'I know you know'."

"Okay, did you say anything back?" Detective Stevenson folded her arms and looked at Detective Williams.

"No, I don't know what to say." Emily assured her.

"Don't worry, I'll tell you what to say. Ask them, 'you know, I know what?'" Emily texted the number and then a response came through.

You know, I know what? Emily texted at 9:08 am.

That I killed your sister. Sent from Andrea's phone at 9:09 am.

"What do I say now?" Emily asked.

"Ask them why they did it," Detective Williams said.

Yes, I do know. But why did you do it? My sister never hurt anyone, Emily texted at 9:10 am.

Because she deserved it for hurting me. Sent from Andrea's phone at 9:11 am.

Emily showed Detective Stevenson and Detective Williams the response.

"Emily, ask them what Andrea did," Detective Stevenson said. "It may help us narrow things down."

What did my sister do to hurt you? Emily asked at 9:13 am.

After waiting a while, there was no response from Andrea's phone.

"No response."

"Don't worry, they're just toying with your emotions," Detective Williams said. "They'll respond again soon."

"Alright, let's go. We'll talk to Samantha and Albert Little today. We'll pay a visit to Veronica and Riley or have them come in and give a statement tomorrow. We'll figure this out," Detective Stevenson said as she and Detective Williams prepared to walk out of the police station. "Emily, stay here. Let Veronica and Riley know that we'll come speak with them tomorrow morning, or they can come here."

The detectives left with a couple officers and headed to Oak Park to speak with Samantha Little. After a thirty-minute drive, they were finally in front of Samantha and Albert's daughter's house. They walked up the stairs and rang the doorbell. A minute later a small, middle-aged white woman, who looked to be 5'2 and 120 pounds came to the door holding an infant.

"May I help you?" the woman asked.

"Hello ma'am. I'm Detective Stevenson and this is Detective Williams. We're looking for Samantha Little?"

"I'm Samantha Little. What seems to be the problem, Detectives?" .

"We're here to ask you questions about your husband, Albert Little," Detective Williams said.

"Is everything alright with Albert?" Samantha asked worried.

"Albert is a suspect in a murder case, ma'am," Detective Stevenson said. "The murder of Andrea Kane."

"Isn't that the name of the girl who was found dead at the construction site?" Samantha Little opened the front door and came out onto the porch.

"Yes ma'am," Detective Williams said.

"Why would Albert be connected to that girl's murder?"

"Because he was one of her sugar daddies," Detective Stevenson said, and Samantha Little's face dropped.

"Oh," Samantha Little responded with eyes wide open in shock.

"Is it okay if we come in and ask you a few questions about Albert's whereabouts and your relationship with him?" Detective Williams asked.

"Yes, of course, come in." Samantha Little opened the door wider so the detectives could come in. "Let me put my granddaughter in her bassinet, you two have a seat in the living room through there."

"Thank you," Detective Williams said as Samantha Little put her granddaughter in her bassinet and then sat down in the living room with the detectives.

"You have a beautiful granddaughter, Ms. Little," Detective Stevenson said.

"Oh, thank you. She's only three months old. I moved in with my daughter and her husband after she told us she was pregnant. I wanted to be closer to them and help her with the baby. This was after the separation. Albert and I agreed to sell the house, so he got his own condo in Chicago close to the hospital and the university."

"How long exactly have you two been separated?" Detective Stevenson asked.

"Oh, well technically we've been separated for years, just living under the same roof for the sake of our children. That didn't really work — it just confused us more. We were constantly angry with one another, but then sparks would fly again. Pretty soon we'd feel the need to try again, but it just never seemed to work. Our youngest son went off to college a couple years ago and that's when I told Albert that we should officially separate. He would stay in another room in the house. I would stay in another room as well. That lasted a few months, then he decided to get an apartment elsewhere. Once my daughter told me she was pregnant I decided that I wanted to be as close to her as possible and help her as much as possible. I moved in right away, and she asked me to stay longer than anticipated. So I told Albert that I wanted to sell the house. He was fine with it since none of us were staying there, and the kids didn't feel the need to keep pretending like we were one big happy family. I moved in with my daughter for good, and I filed for divorce about three weeks ago."

"When you filed for divorce did this come as a shock to Albert?" Detective Stevenson asked.

"No, not at all. He knew eventually I would file, or he would. I guess he was waiting for me to do it. I told him that I wanted a divorce, not just a separation a week before I completed the paperwork. He told me that he knew it was coming and he said that I could do whatever I wanted. He knew that we would never get back together, and that was fine with him. So, I don't think he was surprised at all — we both knew it was coming."

"Did you know that he was seeing anyone?" Detective Williams asked.

"He's a man, we aren't together anymore, and we aren't living together anymore. I knew he had the opportunity and freedom to see someone else now. Albert keeps long hours because he's a surgeon, and he's one of the top surgeons in Chicago. I thought maybe he started dating again, but maybe he didn't because he didn't have much time. Either way, I never knew that he was what you call a 'sugar daddy'" Samantha Little put up air quotes with her fingers when she said sugar daddy.

"Do you know exactly what a sugar daddy is, Ms. Little?" Detective Stevenson asked.

"It's an older man who dates a younger woman, right? And, I assume, gives her money for spending time and having an intimate relationship with him?"

"Pretty much, that's it," Detective Williams said.

"So this girl, Andrea Kane — Albert was her sugar daddy?" Samantha Little asked.

"He was one of her sugar daddies. She had three, actually," Detective Stevenson corrected Samantha Little.

"Oh, well I didn't know Albert could keep up with a girl like that. We're both 62 years old. How old was this young lady?"

"She was 20 years old," Detective Williams said.

"I just don't understand how he would even have the time to devote to this. I mean, he's a surgeon, and he teaches courses from time to time at the university when he's not at the hospital."

"Well, that's what we're trying to figure out ma'am. We were wondering that too," Detective Williams said.

"I just don't understand why he's a suspect."

"It's because he threatened her," Detective Stevenson said.

"What do you mean by threatened?" Samantha Little asked.

"He told her that he wanted to be with her, that he loved her, and he wanted them to become serious. He told her that she could let her other two sugar daddies go and that he would take care of her. She told him she couldn't do that because she had a little sister that she wanted to take care of and she wasn't looking for anything serious," Detective Williams said.

"Then once she didn't accept his offer and denied him, he told her that she'd better break up with the other guys or else. Have you ever known Albert to be violent?" Detective Stevenson asked.

"Heavens, no! Albert is a very sensitive man. I should know, we were married for 38 years. We share three kids and three grandkids together. Albert sounds as if his ego was crushed. You know what that does to men. He'd been using his money to keep this girl close, and he thought he could use his money to make her be devoted to him. Once that didn't work, his ego was crushed, and he became very sensitive. I don't think he would've hurt her, and he definitely wouldn't have killed her. When he said 'or else,' he probably just meant he would cut her off. You know he wouldn't give her any more money. If Albert told this girl that he loved her and wanted to be with her, he wouldn't kill her. He sounds like he wanted to be with her too badly."

"Thank you Ms. Little, that puts things into perspective a bit," Detective Williams said. "Do you know where Albert is now?"

"Let's see, today is Thursday, so he should be at the hospital today. If he isn't, he must've changed his schedule and he's teaching today. If he's not doing either of those, then he's either playing golf or he's at home painting. He's a very simple man."

"Thank you ma'am. Here is my card, call us if you need or find out anything." Detective Stevenson handed Samantha Little her card.

"No problem, and thank you. I'll walk you two out." Samantha Little escorted the detectives to the front porch.

The detectives got into the car and headed to the University of Illinois in Chicago hospital to see if Albert Little was there. They didn't want to take him away from work, but they didn't want him to react hysterically and run away either. Once they were inside the hospital the detectives started to come up with a plan. This was their last suspect, and they needed this to work.

"Good morning ma'am, we're detectives and we're here for Albert Little," Detective Stevenson said, showing his badge to the receptionist at the front desk.

“Yes, Albert Little’s office is on the fifth floor. He has a surgery scheduled in a couple hours,” the receptionist responded.

“A couple hours is all we need. Thank you.”

“I’ll let him know you’re here to see him,” the receptionist said as she picked up the phone.

“No need, we’ll just make our way upstairs,” Detective Stevenson said as she and Detective Williams walked to the elevator.

“You think he’ll be cooperative?” Detective Williams asked while they were on the elevator.

“I think he should be, I mean, he’s the last person I thought would be the murderer.” The detectives exited the elevator on the fifth floor.

“Hi, we’re detectives, and we’re here to see Dr. Albert Little. Is he in his office?” Detective Williams asked the receptionist on the fifth floor as they showed their badges.

“Yes, his office is straight that way. It’s the second door on the right-hand side,” the receptionist told the detectives as she led them to the office.

“Thank you.” They walked to Albert Little’s door, worried that Albert may not be there, or that he may not want to talk.

Knock. Knock. Knock.

The receptionist knocked on the door.

"Dr. Little, it's Angela," the receptionist said.

Albert Little opened the door, and he wasn't at all what the detectives were expecting. A short, 5'7, middle-aged man with gray hair and glasses. He had on a sweater, a button-down shirt, and khakis. He was holding a golf club in his hand as he answered the door. He looked like a sweet and pleasant grandfather.

"Hi Angela, how are you?" Albert moved in towards Angela and kissed her on the cheek. This surprised the detectives, as they wondered *when did professors start kissing their receptionists on the cheek.*

"Hi Dr. Little, you have a couple visitors here to see you," Angela said.

"May I help you?" Albert Little asked.

"I'm Detective Stevenson and this is Detective Williams. We're here to ask you some questions about Andrea Kane."

"Please come into my office," Albert Little said quickly, looking startled as he opened the door wide so the detectives could enter and beckoned Angela to go back to her post. The detectives couldn't help but notice that Albert had a nice clean office, with many books.

Classical music was playing in the background, everything was well organized, and there was an indoor golf set right in the middle of the room in front of his desk and guest chairs. "I don't want anyone to hear about my personal business. Please have a seat. Is everything okay with Andrea?"

"No sir, we thought you knew by now. Andrea Kane was found murdered at a construction site of a high-rise condo building," Detective Stevenson said as Albert Little stared at them in disbelief. He took off his glasses, wiped his eyes, and sat down. He was the first of her sugar daddies to cry when the detectives announced her death. "We're sorry you had to hear this way. We thought you knew."

"Do… do you know who murdered her?" Albert Little asked in a soft voice while he kept wiping his eyes.

"We don't know, sir, we're trying to figure that out," Detective Williams said. "It has come to our knowledge that you had a relationship with Andrea Kane."

"Yes, we know that you were one of her sugar daddies," Detective Stevenson said as Albert Little finally looked back up at them from his chair behind his desk.

"I was," Albert responded.

"Dr. Little, when was the last time you saw Andrea Kane?" Detective Stevenson asked.

"It was January 15th-17th. We went to Wisconsin and stayed in a little cabin out there for a weekend. I just wanted to spend some time with her since I had spent so much time with family over the holidays. It was the only time I could get away with her."

"Did she seem fine when you all spent time together?" Detective Williams asked.

"Yes, she was perfectly fine. Just as charismatic and beautiful as ever. We had a wonderful time in our cabin. She said she enjoyed not being in the city for a little bit."

"So you didn't see or hear from her any time after that?" Detective Williams asked.

"No, I haven't heard from her since then. I told her that I would be very busy at the hospital and at the university. Andrea was very respectful, so she would usually wait for me to call her or contact her. I did send her money a couple of times. A few hundred dollars to her account. That was on the 20th and on the 22nd. She didn't ask me to —I just wanted to send her something since we had such a good time at the cabin."

"So you haven't received a text message or anything from her since then?" Detective Stevenson asked.

"No, I'm afraid not," Albert Little said.

"Dr. Little, tell us how you and Andrea met," Detective Williams said.

"It's a very long and complicated story…" Albert began before he was interrupted.

"Please, we have nothing but time. Finding out who murdered Andrea depends on it," Detective Williams said.

"Am I a suspect because of our relationship?" Albert asked alarmed.

"Well, your name came up because the homicide seemed to be domestic. And we know that you were in a relationship with Andrea," Detective Stevenson said. "We just want to hear your side of the story so your name can be cleared."

"Okay. Well, my wife and I had been going through some things all throughout our marriage…"

"What sort of things?" Detective Williams asked.

"We fell out of love. She felt that I didn't spend enough time with her and our children. I spent a lot of time being a surgeon and professor. I was working towards my goal of being one of the best surgeons in Chicago. I guess I forgot about my family trying to accomplish this goal. My wife had fallen out of love with me a long time ago. We stayed together for our children. Once our youngest son left for college, we decided to separate for good. I would move out of our home and she could stay there if she wanted to. I never wanted her to do anything she didn't want to do. Even though I knew it was inevitable, I loved my wife dearly, and I wanted us to work. I wanted us to be together. I missed having her in my life, but I knew that she didn't want to be with me anymore.

"Andrea and I started talking just this August after my son headed back to school, my daughter announced her pregnancy, and my ex-wife told me she wanted me to sell the house. I felt very lonely, and I decided that I should get a girlfriend, you know, maybe a woman to spend some time with, or who would be there when I got home. A friend of mine told me about this app where older men could connect with younger women who were looking for someone to take care of them. I never knew what a sugar daddy was, or that I would become one. On the site there were many girls you could connect with, but one girl in particular stood out to me. It was Andrea. All the girls were beautiful, but she was the most beautiful. I decided to reach out to her. We talked for a bit through the app, and then I asked her if she would like to meet for dinner. A week later we met for dinner. I was nervous — I hadn't been out on a date with a woman besides my wife for a long time. Andrea told me there was no need for me to be nervous. She made me feel at ease. We had a wonderful time, and I told her that I would like to see her again. She said she was fine with that. So we talked and we went on more dates. Andrea would come over from time-to-time. I really just liked her company more than anything."

"So how did you make time for her?" Detective Williams asked. "You know, with you being one of the top surgeons in Chicago and a professor."

"I didn't have as much time as I would've liked to have with her. We saw each other maybe once or twice a month. We never went anywhere besides Wisconsin together."

"Is that when you told her that you loved her and you wanted to be with her?" Detective Stevenson asked. Albert Little looked shocked when he heard this and wondered how the detectives knew about that.

"Yes, that's when I told her that," Albert said.

“Did you also tell her to break up with her other sugar daddies?” Detective Williams asked.

“Yes, I did. I told her that I wanted us to be together and that she didn’t need them. I told her that I would take care of her,” Albert started to twiddle his fingers. He was nervous because he could tell that the detectives were suspicious of him.

“Did you also tell her that she had better break up with them or else?” Detective Stevenson said. Albert Little looked at both detectives for a moment, and then he lowered his head.

“Yes. Yes, I did tell her that. That’s why you’re both here, isn't it?” Albert asked.

“Dr. Little, what did you mean by that ‘or else’?” Detective Williams asked.

“I meant that I would cut her off. I would stop seeing her. When she told me she had three sugar daddies, she said it was because none of the relationships were consistent. She told me that’s why she never complained when I said that I was too busy, or away with my family, or that I didn’t have time — because she was used to it, and there was always another sugar daddy to be around. She said she would just make time with another sugar daddy and that she wasn’t looking for anything serious. I was furious when she told me this. I thought Andrea and I were serious, that she was my girlfriend. I didn't realize that I was sharing her with two other men."

"So you made the relationship more serious than she did?" Detective Williams asked.

"Yes, I guess so. When I signed up on this site, I thought it was like a dating site. I thought that even though I was signing up to be her sugar daddy, we would eventually establish a relationship. I had dreams of us moving in together, getting married, things like that."

"With a 20-year-old girl that you met from a dating app?" Detective Williams asked, in a judgemental, disgusted, and confused tone.

"I know it was a bit much to ask for, but that's how I felt. She told me she didn't want anything serious. That she had her little sister to take care of. I became upset, I thought she was just rejecting me. I thought, *How could a young woman who was so beautiful truly want to be with me?* So I became upset, and I told her that she'd better break up with them or else. I said this on our last day at the cabin. I felt bad about it and thought that maybe she didn't want to talk to me anymore. That's why I sent her the money I felt guilty. I tried calling her, but she didn't answer her phone," Albert Little said.

"When was the last time you tried calling her?" Detective Stevenson asked.

"January 25th," Albert Little responded.

"Dr. Little, where were you on January 28th and 29th?" Detective Williams asked. "Andrea's autopsy revealed that her time of death was around that time. We need to know what you were doing and where you were on those days?"

"Let me look at my calendar." Albert Little pulled up his calendar on his computer. "Let me see… I had back to back surgeries on the 28th. Then after that I went home to get some sleep. The 29th, the same thing. Only I had a class to teach that night. I went home after teaching the class."

"And you want to tell us a little bit more about your relationship with your receptionist, Angela?" Detective Stevenson asked.

"Yes, um…Angela and I have been seeing each other. After the blow-up with Andrea and not hearing from her, I decided to ask out Angela. I had always admired her beauty, and she's not as young as

Andrea. She's around 45 and she wants something a bit more serious," Albert Little responded.

"How much longer after the blow-up with Andrea?" Detective Williams asked.

"I'd say about a week," Albert said.

"Okay, those are all the questions we have for you, for now. Thank you," Detective Stevenson said as she and Detective Williams stood up to walk out of Albert's office.

"Excuse me," Albert Little said, and the detectives turned around. "Please find the person who did this to Andrea. She was a very kind girl, and she didn't deserve this."

"Thank you. We keep hearing that, but it seems that someone wanted her gone," Detective Stevenson said as they exited Albert's office. Once out in the hallway, she glanced at Angela. She couldn't help but feel that it wasn't a coincidence that she started dating Albert once everything happened with Andrea, and then Andrea came up dead.

"Angela," Detective Stevenson began to say. "Do you know anything about the young girl who's dead body was left at a construction site?"

"No, I don't. Besides what I saw on the news. Is that why you're all here? Was the girl a student here?" Angela responded looking confused and afraid.

"No she wasn't, she had a connection to Albert…" Detective Stevenson said before Detective Williams cut her off.

"Stevie." He gave her a look as if to say, *Don't you dare give any extra information.*

"You should ask him, here's my card if you find anything." Detective Stevenson said to Angela before she and Detective Williams walked away.

Both the detectives went downstairs to make sure Albert Little was telling the truth. It turned out he had performed back-to-back surgeries on the 28th and the 29th. The detectives drove over to the university and found that Albert also taught a class on the 29th. They headed back to the car feeling defeated and not wanting to go to the police station just yet. They knew the chief would be upset, and they knew based on his conversation that they had better come up with something before heading back.

"What are you thinking about?" Detective Williams asked.

“About everything, it’s just not adding up. Everyone who we thought could’ve done it, were nowhere around Andrea at her time of death,” Detective Stevenson said rubbing her head.

“Yeah, I know.”

“Albert wanted to be in a committed relationship with Andrea so badly, but then having this pop up girlfriend who works at his office just doesn’t add up either.”

“Yeah, I know.”

“The last time anyone saw Andrea was when Calvin left for D.C.” A silence came over the car. Then Detective Stevenson said, “That’s it!”

“What’s it?”

“I don’t know why I didn’t think of it before. We need to ask the Uber driver. We need to ask the Uber driver where they dropped Andrea off the day she was killed.”

“Yeah, but I don’t have the license plate number or make and model of the vehicle.”

“We can try calling Calvin Bruno, or we can go back to the airport.”

“No need to call, Calvin doesn’t live too far from here. Let’s drive over to his place, see if he’s there.” They sped off to go back to Calvin Bruno’s loft building. Once they entered the building they showed their badges to the security desk and took the elevator back up to Calvin’s loft apartment. The security guard looked their way and didn’t say anything.

Knock. Knock. Knock.

“Calvin, this is Detective Williams and Detective Stevenson. Open up.” Calvin opened the door a few minutes later.

“Yes, Detectives?” Calvin whispered as he peeked through the door.

“Can we come in?” Detective Stevenson asked.

“No, I’ll come out there, I have company,” Calvin whispered again. “Give me a second, honey,” the detectives heard Calvin say before he stepped out into the hallway wearing only briefs and throwing on his robe.

“Is Lily in there? I thought she said she was done with you,” Detective Stevenson said.

“Oh no, that’s not Lily.” Calvin smirked as he shook his head.

"Look — never mind. We don't need to know. We just came by to ask the make, model, and license plate number of the Uber you and Andrea took to the airport that day," Detective Williams asked.

"Oh, you think the Uber driver might be able to tell you where they dropped her off that day?" Calvin asked. "That's funny, I thought you all would've done that by now," he said sarcastically as he went back into his loft to get his phone. He left Detective Williams and Detective Stevenson standing there looking dumbfounded. When he came back, he said, "Okay, the make and model of the car was a black Honda HR-V sport. The license plate number was F228892."

"Thank you, sorry to interrupt whatever you have going on," Detective Williams said as Detective Stevenson walked back to the elevator.

"No problem, anything to help find Andrea's killer," Calvin said before he went back into his place.

"Okay, so let's head back to the station and tell the chief and Emily about our interrogations with Albert and Samantha Little. We'll let them know that we saw Calvin and got the make, model, and license plate number for the car of the Uber driver," Detective Stevenson said while she and Detective Williams were on the elevator.

"While you're explaining everything I'll start looking for the Uber driver."

"Sounds good to me, partner." Detective Stevenson smiled as she looked at Detective Williams. She was starting to feel like she and Williams were back to their old selves again. This is how they worked, quick on their feet with their minds and bodies moving at the exact same pace.

Back at the police station, the chief was sitting in his office when he saw them walk in.

"Williams, Stevenson, what's going on?" the chief asked sternly as Emily walked in from the waiting area because she'd heard the chief say their names.

"Chief, I have to look something up, but Stevie will explain everything," Detective Williams said as he walked over to his computer.

"Chief, we talked to Albert and Samantha Little. Samantha never knew about Andrea Kane. Albert had seen her from time to time and wanted things to get more serious. He threatened to cut her off and not see her again. That's why he told her 'or else'. He had back-to-back surgeries and he had to teach classes at the university both days that Andrea could've died. So we figured out that he couldn't have done it. Just as Williams and I felt we had hit another wall we thought we should get the Uber driver's information. You know, the one who drove Andrea and Calvin to the airport and then drove Andrea somewhere else. That would be the last person that saw her."

"And so? Did you go by the airport to get that information?" the chief asked.

"No need, we went by Calvin Bruno's place, and he told us the make and model of the vehicle and license plate number. Williams is putting it into the system. Where is Emily, Chief?" Detective Stevenson asked.

"I'm right here." Emily came towards Detective Stevenson.

"Oh good, Emily, you're still here," Detective Stevenson said taking a breath.

"Yeah, and I heard everything you said," Emily responded.

"Stevie, I found the vehicle owner. It's a man by the name Victor Santiago. He got a speeding ticket a couple months ago. He lives in the Pilsen neighborhood. I have his address, let's go," Detective

Williams said as he and Detective Stevenson started leaving the police station.

"You see, Emily, that's a real detective. Quick with your mind, and quick on your feet," the chief said proudly as the two detectives left the police station.

The detectives drove to the Uber driver's house in Pilsen. They saw the car sitting outside. Luckily, he was home, they both thought.

Knock. Knock. Knock.

"Who is it?" a voice from behind the door asked.

"This is Detective Williams and Detective Stevenson, we're looking for Victor Santiago." The door began to open, and there was a small Latina woman standing in the doorway.

"Hello Detectives, Victor isn't here," the woman who answered the door said.

"I'm sorry ma'am, we saw his car sitting right there, so we thought he might be home," Detective Stevenson said.

"No, he's not home right now. He's still at work. Is everything okay? I'm his wife, Maria," the woman said.

"Everything is fine. It's just that we're investigating a murder, and we understand that Victor drives Uber…" Detective Williams said.

"Victor doesn't drive Uber, I do. The car is registered in his name, but I drive Uber some mornings while my kids are at school and while Victor is at work. I do it to make some extra money for our family," Maria explained.

"Oh, well you're the person we need to talk to, then. Do you remember this girl and this man?" Detective Stevenson asked as she showed Maria Santiago a picture of Andrea and Calvin. "You took this girl to the airport with this man on January 28th at 10:00 am?"

"Yeah, I remember. I thought he was her father because he was so much older than her. But it turns out they were a couple."

"That young lady is Andrea Kane. She's our murder victim," Detective Williams said.

"Really?" Maria asked in shock and sadness.

"Yes, her autopsy revealed that she was murdered either the day she was with you or the next day," Detective Williams said.

“Do you remember where you dropped her off that day after you left the airport?” Detective Stevenson asked as Maria stepped onto the porch and closed the door.

“My mother is in there, I don’t want her to hear. She’ll be all up in our business, telling everyone in the neighborhood. This is better than her telenovellas. I dropped the girl off at a Starbucks downtown. Like on Michigan Avenue. She didn’t talk much at first. I just asked her where she wanted to go, and she said she was going to go to Starbucks and go shopping. So she wanted me to take her on the Magnificent Mile so she could shop. I told her that it sounded like a fun morning to me. You know, I always try to talk to my passengers, especially when we’re going to be driving for a long time. Coming from the airport to the Magnificent Mile at 10:00 am was going to be a long drive. So I asked her if that guy who was in the car with us was her husband. She said he was her boyfriend, and he was going to a conference in D.C. I told her he looked a lot older than her. She said she was 20 and he was in his early 50’s. She said he was a doctor and professor who made a lot of money. So I told her I could see why she was with him. Not to mention he was good looking too. You know, he was one of those silver foxes, as people say. An older man with nice looks," Maria went on.

"Anyway, she told me she had lived here in Chicago all her life with her sister and everything. I asked her if her family was okay with her dating a man that was much older than her. She said that they weren't, but it wasn't that serious. I told her my mother would've killed me if I dated a man that much older than me when I was her age, even if he did have a lot of money and looked that good. I asked her if he treated her well, and she said yeah. She told me she liked the sunglasses I was wearing. I told her that my husband gave them to me as a birthday present. She told me she had a pair just like them. Then we talked about clothes, shopping, and stores that we liked to go to. I don't wear a lot of designer clothes, but she was telling me about all of the nice places she likes to shop. We started talking about traveling, and she told me she went to Dubai and Mauritius with her boyfriend. I told her I wanted to go there one day. Stuff like that. Then I dropped her off at Starbucks on the Magnificent Mile. That was it."

"Do you remember if she met up with anyone when you dropped her off?" Detective Williams asked.

"No I don't, I'm sorry," Maria said.

"Okay, well that doesn't give us a lot to go off of, but at least we know you all stopped at a Starbucks downtown. We can go from there," Detective Stevenson said.

"Yeah, I'm sorry. I feel so bad. Now I wished I wouldn't have dropped her off. Maybe she'd still be here, you know?" Maria responded sadly.

"Yeah, I know what you mean," Detective Stevenson said. "Thank you anyway for your cooperation."

"Of course, I hope you all find out who killed her. She seemed like a nice girl. Driving Uber you just never know who is in the car with you. Like, I dropped that girl off at Starbucks, and she became a murder victim. Give my condolences to her family." Maria went back into her house.

"We will, thank you," Detective Williams said before he and Detective Stevenson walked back to the car. "I hate that we gotta tell Emily and the chief this."

"Me too," Detective Stevenson said.

They drove back to the police station feeling defeated. Back at the station, Emily was sitting in a chair next to Detective Willams' desk.

"Emily, you're still here?" Detective Stevenson asked.

“Yeah, I wanted to see what the Uber driver said. So where did they drop Andrea off?”

“They dropped her off at a Starbucks on the Magnificent Mile. Nothing that really tells us anything. I’m sorry, Emily,” Detective Williams said.

“Don’t be, you guys have done so much for Andrea and me. Hopefully, maybe Veronica and Riley can tell you something tomorrow.”

“Hey, did the person ever text you back from Andrea’s phone?” Detective Stevenson asked.

“No, not at all.”

“Why don’t you try texting them back. Resend them what you texted them before to show that you’re waiting for a response from them,” Detective Stevenson said.

“Okay.” Emily texted the number again.

Ding. Ding. A message finally came through.

What did my sister do to hurt you? Emily texted at 5:30 pm.

She was with the man I loved. Sent from Andrea’s phone at 5:31 pm.

Emily showed the detectives the messages.

"Well, that doesn't narrow it down," Detective Williams said.

"No, maybe it does."

"How? Amber Wright and Lily Bostitch had an alibi," Emily responded.

"I know, but hear me out. Nicholas Wright's nanny and his wife said he had many girlfriends. I think he may have had a romantic relationship with his receptionist. Calvin Bruno said himself that he had many girlfriends too. When we went over to his house today there was a woman there and he said it wasn't Lily. Albert also had a romantic relationship with the receptionist at his office. So maybe it's one of the girlfriends."

"But Calvin had Lily, and people knew they were an item. So why come after Andrea if you're not going to go after Lily?" Detective Williams asked.

"Yeah, that doesn't make sense," Emily said shrugging her shoulders.

"Okay, so maybe it's one of Nicholas' girlfriends or maybe Albert's new girlfriend. Maybe they killed Andrea."

"Yeah, but that doesn't narrow anything down. We don't know how many there are and none of those women could've transported

Andrea's body to the construction site by themselves. A man had to help them transport the body, so now I think we're looking for two people," Detective Williams said.

"Okay, well maybe that can be the next thing we find out. We'll pay a visit to Veronica and Riley tomorrow, and then maybe we can ask Nicholas Wright about his dating history," Detective Stevenson hoped.

"Do you think he'd be willing to give us that information?" Detective Williams asked.

"Maybe. I mean, that might explain how Andrea's body ended up at his construction site."

"Okay, but that still doesn't explain how Andrea got from the Magnificent Mile to the construction site in West Loop," Emily said.

"I know, but maybe the girls can share their information tomorrow. We can talk to Nicholas Wright, and then we can piece everything together. We can also ask the receptionist who's dating Albert Little some questions," Detective Stevenson placed her hand on Emily's shoulder to assure her that this was a good plan.

"Williams and Stevenson, how did everything go with the Uber driver?" the chief asked, walking up to Detective Williams' desk.

"Well Chief, we found the Uber driver, but they dropped Andrea off at a Starbucks on the Magnificent Mile," Detective Williams said.

"Well that's a dead end. So how did the victim end up getting shot four times, frozen, and placed at her sugar daddy's construction site?" The chief asked.

"I don't know, Chief, that's what we're trying to figure out. But the person texted Emily back, they told her that Andrea slept with the man she loved. That's why they killed her," Detective Stevenson said.

"So we think it's a woman?" the chief asked. "But we already questioned all of the women connected to the men."

"Not all of them, Chief. Both Calvin and Nicholas had multiple partners," Detective Williams said. "And we found out today that Albert is dating his receptionist."

"But we excluded Calvin because of Lily. If someone were going to kill Andrea it would make sense for them to come after Lily too," Detective Stevenson said.

"So you think it's one of Nicholas Wright's girlfriends or Albert Little's new squeeze?"

"Yeah. We'll try to see if he wants to share any information about this tomorrow after we talk to Andrea's friends, Veronica and Riley," Detective Stevenson said.

"And we also plan to ask Albert's new girlfriend some questions," Detective Williams added.

"Okay, well that sounds like a plan to me. Good work you three," the chief said to the two detectives and Emily. Emily blushed as the chief walked away.

"Good work Emily, we couldn't have gotten this far without you," Detective Williams said, winking at Emily as he walked away.

"Thanks." Emily blushed even more.

"So where are you staying tonight, kid?" Detective Stevenson asked. "Are you going with Ms. Baker or with the girls?"

"You know, I think I'll go home. Back to me and Dre's place."

"Are you sure you're ready for that?"

"Yeah. Can you come with me?"

"Yeah, of course. I'll drive you there and come in with you. Make sure everything is good," Detective Stevenson said. Afterwards, Detective Stevenson walked to her car and Emily walked to Andrea's car to head to Andrea's place. Once they were outside the building,

Emily parked in Andrea's parking spot, and Detective Stevenson found street parking in front of the building. Both ladies entered the elevator to head to Andrea's apartment.

"How is your school work coming along?" Detective Stevenson asked.

"Oh, I was able to catch up on a lot of my work today when I was at the station while you and Detective Williams were gone. I told the chief that I've been missing school and didn't want to get behind on my work. He gave me a laptop, a pen and pad, and sat me in an interrogation room so I could get my work done. He's not so bad once you get to know him," Emily said.

"I'm glad you were able to see that side of him. The chief is a sweet guy, he just doesn't want anybody to know it. Don't tell him I told you that. He'd kill me." They exited the elevator and walked up to Andrea's apartment door. Emily was shaking a bit as she put the key in the lock and opened the door. She walked into Andrea's apartment and just stood still as she looked around the living room and kitchen. She stood there while Detective Stevenson looked around the apartment to make sure nothing seemed off. Andrea's apartment was open concept like Detective Stevenson's, but her apartment was clean, decorated, comfortable, and homey, with pictures of her, Emily, Mama Kim, and their grandmother all over the place. Andrea couldn't cook, but there were smells of different candles in the apartment. There were also two bedrooms instead of one. Emily seemed to be blank for a moment.

"Emily, you okay?" Detective Stevenson asked.

"Yeah…yeah, I'll be fine," Emily wiped a few tears from her face with her sleeve.

"I looked around, and everything seemed okay to me."

"Thank you." Emily sat on the sofa.

"No problem. You'll be happy to know I took your advice. I cleaned up my place, did some laundry, washed dishes, and even made myself breakfast this morning. Nothing big, just coffee, toast, and eggs. It felt good to get a little organized." Detective Stevenson could tell Emily was teary and tried to cheer her up.

"That's great, I'm happy for you. I knew it would feel good." Emily grinned.

"Thank you. I can understand why you felt like my place was lacking so much. You and Andrea's place is nice, you know, for a 20 and 18 year old."

“Thanks, that was all Andrea. She had an eye for nice things, I guess.”

“I also took some more of your advice. I went out to a bar last night, and I met someone there.”

“Did you?” Emily said excitedly. “Another officer?”

“No, not another officer. We actually have a date tonight at seven,” Detective Stevenson said, blushing.

“That’s great. Well you better hurry home so you can get ready.”

“What do you mean get ready?”

“I know you’re not wearing that on your date,” Emily said disgustedly. “You’ve been out running around the city all day. You’re sweaty and you look exhausted. You need a nice outfit. C’mon, it’s my turn to give you something to wear.” Emily walked into her room and pulled a large box from her closet.

“Emily, no, I can’t. I can’t take any of you or Andrea’s clothes.”

“Yes, you can. Here, this is a dress Dre gave me. She thought I would like it, but I’m not into all that stuff.” Emily opened a box with a nice white dress in it. “It’ll look great on you. Go try it on.”

“Emily, I can’t take this. This was a gift to you from Andrea.”

"And I want to give it to you. Just take it as a gift for all you've done for me these past few days."

"Okay." Detective Stevenson delicately grabbed the dress from the box and went into the lavender-scented bathroom to change into it. She put it on and felt out of place. This was completely different from her slacks, button down shirt, badge, and gun. She stepped out of the bathroom to show Emily.

"You look fantastic already." Emily was surprised. "I have never seen you like this. I have some heels that'll look great with this."

"Emily, c'mon."

"Please? This is making me feel better. Now put the shoes on," Emily commanded.

"Okay." Detective Stevenson put the shoes on after Emily's forceful push. Emily was shocked that Detective Stevenson even knew how to walk in heels.

"There is a full-length mirror in Andrea's room. You should go check yourself out. You look great." Detective Stevenson stepped into Andrea's room and looked at herself in the full-length mirror. Emily stopped and stood in the doorway and looked around Andrea's room.

"I like it, Emily, thank you. Emily?" Detective Stevenson saw Emily standing in the doorway of Andrea's room through the mirror.

"I… I haven't been in here in a while. It feels weird being in her room when she's not here."

"Emily, are you sure you want to stay here? Maybe you should go back to Ms. Baker's place." Detective Stevenson walked over to Emily.

"No, I think I should stay here," Emily cried while looking around.

Detective Stevenson paused for a moment as she stared at Emily. Her heart began to race and she felt a strong pain in her stomach. She walked over to Emily and grabbed her shoulders.

"What's wrong?" Emily asked.

"Emily, did Andrea take her keys with her when she left that morning on the 28th?"

"Yeah, why?"

"Because, there were no keys on her when we found her body. So that means that whoever has her phone has her keys as well. Were her car keys attached too?"

"Yeah."

“We have to get you out of here. Let me get my clothes back on and we’ll go back downstairs. You have to stay at Ms. Baker’s house tonight.” Detective Stevenson ran back to the bathroom frantically to change clothes and get Emily out of the apartment.

“But how would they know where we lived? Andrea’s I.D. still had the address to the apartment she stayed in with Veronica and Riley.”

“That doesn’t matter. They still could've figured out where she lives.” Detective Stevenson got dressed, put her badge and gun back on, and escorted Emily to her car. They drove to Ms. Baker’s home, and Detective Stevenson sat in her car and watched Emily go into Ms. Baker’s house. Detective Stevenson then called Detective Williams before she went on her date.

“Yo, Stevie, what’s up?” Detective Williams asked.

“Williams, Emily and I drove to Andrea’s place. I looked around the place for her, but I didn’t find anything suspicious. But she told me today that Andrea took her house and car keys with her that morning. That means that whoever has her phone, has her keys as well.”

“Good thinking Stevie, so what do you want to do?” Detective Williams asked.

"Tomorrow, after we talk to Andrea's friends, I'll have Emily go back to Andrea's house. I think we should make it look like she came by herself. I'll have her stay in the apartment, park the car, all of that. We'll have officers standing around in regular clothes. Emily will text the person and try to get some more information out of them. I'm sure this person knows where Andrea lived as well. They could've been in her apartment all this time Emily has been gone. They may have cameras in there and everything. Emily will stay there all night. She'll text us, but I'm sure eventually the person will try to come over. I'll have Emily tell the person she knows who they are, even though we don't know. Emily will tell them that she's going to tell the police who they are."

"You think that'll work?"

"It's worth a try. I already shared the plan with Emily, and we'll tell the chief tomorrow,"

"Well I'm down, Stevie. Do you still want to talk to Andrea's friends tomorrow? It seems like you have a pretty solid plan."

"Yeah, they said they had something to tell us, so I want to know what it is before we do this tomorrow."

“Okay, well, I’ll see you tomorrow. Are Andrea’s friends coming to us, or are we going to them?”

“I told Emily to tell them to come to the police station tomorrow.”

“Okay. Cheryl made pot roast tonight if you want to swing by?”

“Uh, I can’t tonight,” Detective Stevenson said, grinning from ear to ear.

“Why, you going back to the station to look some things over?”

“No, I…I have a date.” Detective Stevenson was still grinning as she told Detective Williams the good news.

“You got a date?” Detective Williams laughed. “Well go ‘head, Stevie, with who? Do I know him?”

“You know you laughing a lil’ bit too hard. And you might know him.”

“Oooooo, alright, um…is he an officer?”

“No, goodbye Williams.” Detective Stevenson hung up the phone. She drove back to her place to take a shower and put on the dress and heels that Emily had given to her for her date. She combed her hair, put on a bit of makeup as well, and then she headed out to meet her date.

Part 4: The Friends

Chapter 7 - Veronica Bridges & Riley Mensa

After her date last night, Detective Stevenson felt incredible. She hadn't realized how much she needed to clean her place, spend time with someone she liked, and get herself organized. She owed it all to Emily, the 18-year-old foster kid whose sister was the victim of a homicide. The next morning, she drove to the police station to meet Emily and Detective Williams. Andrea's friends Veronica and Riley had promised to come to the police station to give their statement, and Detective Stevenson hoped that they would keep their word. She parked in front of the police station, all smiles from her date last night. Emily's car was outside, but this time, Emily was already inside the police station talking with Detective Williams. Detective Stevenson was thrilled they had made up, but she had a strong feeling they were talking about her. As soon as she walked over to Detective Williams' desk, the conversation between Emily and the detective ceased. At that moment, Detective Stevenson knew that they actually had been talking about her.

"Good morning, you two. This is a surprise, you all talking to each other," Detective Stevenson said as she walked up to Emily and Detective Williams.

"Yeah, Emily was telling me all about how she gave you a makeover at Andrea's place for your…date," Detective Williams whispered, emphasizing the word date as Emily stood there, smiling brightly. Detective Stevenson had never seen Emily smile so big.

"Emily, my little makeover was between us," Detective Stevenson whispered so no one else would hear.

"Well, Detective Williams asked me if I knew about it. I guessed that you had told him you were going on a date, so I told him about the makeover. I didn't know it was a secret."

"It's fine, I'm just teasing. There are no secrets between Williams and I."

"Yeah, and judging by that smile on your face, Stevie, I'd say you had a pretty great time. So spit it out, tell us about it. Who is he? Where did y'all go? What did y'all do?" Detective Williams leaned back in his chair.

"Yeah, we're dying to hear about it." Emily smiled as she was sitting in the seat next to Detective Williams' desk.

"I gotta talk to the chief about the plan for today," Detective Stevenson tried to change the subject as she walked away to talk to the chief.

"Oh, c'mon, Stevie."

Knock. Knock. Knock.

"Stevenson?" the chief said after Detective Stevenson knocked on his door.

"Chief, I have a plan for catching the person who has Andrea Kane's phone," Detective Stevenson said.

"Okay, have a seat and close the door," the chief said.

"Okay. So it turns out that Andrea Kane's keys weren't on her when we found her body, but Emily informed me that she took her keys with her that morning when she left. So the person who has her phone should also have her keys. Keys to her car and to her apartment."

"Does the person know what kind of car Andrea drives?"

"We don't know for sure. Andrea had caught an Uber downtown to a Starbucks on the Magnificent Mile, so when they murdered her, she didn't have her car. I'm thinking that maybe now that they know that Emily knows about Andrea's death, Emily can get them to come to Andrea's place."

"Why would they do that?"

"What do you mean, Chief?"

"Why would they come to Andrea's place? They had her keys for two weeks when she was dead at an abandoned construction site, and they never came to pay a visit to Emily. Why would they come now?"

"I know, but this time Emily will lure them in. Andrea never told any of her sugar daddies where she stayed. So the woman who killed Andrea, and whoever helped her move the body, might not know where she stayed either."

"But what about identification, did Andrea have her I.D. card on her when she was murdered?"

"Yes, but Emily told me that the address that was listed on her I.D. was the address where she stayed with her roommates, not her new address."

"Okay, Stevenson, listen. You want to use Emily to contact the person who has the phone, who is possibly the murderer, get them to come to the house, and then trap them. Am I following?"

"Yes."

"But why would the murderer do that? Why would they just come to Emily? Just because she knows now?"

"Because Emily is going to tell the person on the other end of the phone that she knows who they are. She's going to tell them that if they don't return the phone and keys to her, she's going to report them to us. That way the person will be scared."

"And what if that doesn't work?"

"Then we come up with another plan."

"But what if you get this person to flee? We don't know who they are. There was no DNA on Andrea Kane. All of the sugar daddies and their wives and girlfriends checked out. You met with the Uber driver, and they checked out too. The only thing you're depending on is Emily, her phone, and an empty threat because we don't know who this person is. It could be any one of Nicholas Wright's or Calvin Bruno's girlfriends. It could be Albert's new girlfriend. If we're being completely honest, Andrea Kane was a sugar baby, so she could've had another sugar daddy, and she could've been going to meet up with him that day. A woman connected to this new person could've killed her. For all we know it could be a man who killed Andrea at the end of that phone pretending to be a woman. We don't know. Get your head in the game, Stevenson. Think, and stop coming up with these idiotic plans."

"Yes, Chief."

"You said Andrea's friends were coming to give a statement. Get their statement first, and then go from there. Get out of my office." The smile that Detective Stevenson had worn when she entered the police station had disappeared. She walked back over to Detective Williams' desk after exiting the chief's office.

"Well, Stevie, I've known you long enough to know that face is not a good one." Detective Stevenson cut her eyes at him when he made this remark.

"I didn't mean it like that, Stevie," Detective Williams said, holding his hands up.

"So the chief didn't like the plan?" Emily asked.

"Not even a little bit. He said that he feels that the person won't actually show up to Andrea's place. They'd be suspicious."

"Even if I told them that I know who they are?" Emily asked.

"The chief thinks that they'll realize it's an empty threat, and they may try to flee. He also feels that we could not be dealing with a woman. That it could be a man who killed Andrea pretending to be a woman. She could've had another sugar daddy, or she could've been going to meet someone when she went downtown and then was murdered."

"That's not true, she would've told me that. She would've told me if she was going to see a new sugar daddy."

"I know, Emily, and I'm sorry. We'll come up with a different plan," Detective Stevenson said trying to calm Emily down.

"Why is he so doubtful of my sister and I…" Emily asked.

"Emily, lower your voice, or the chief will tell you to go home," Detective Williams whispered.

"I just don't understand. Why can't we go with that plan?" Emily asked frantically.

"Emily, we'll figure this..." Detective Stevenson began to say before she was interrupted.

"Emily. Emily!" Two girls started yelling Emily's name. A police officer stood in front of the girls holding them back and looking at Detective Stevenson for confirmation that the girls could come in.

"Emily, you know those girls?" Detective Williams asked.

"That's Veronica and Riley, they're here to give their statement," Emily said.

"Okay, let's place them in an interrogation room for their statement," Detective Stevenson told the officer holding the girls back. "Williams, you ready?"

"Yeah, I'll tell the chief so he and Emily can stand behind the window," Detective Williams said walking to the chief's office.

The detectives walked inside of the interrogation room where Riley and Veronica sat patiently waiting for them to enter. The chief and Emily stood behind the window to watch.

"Riley, Veronica, thank you for coming in to give this statement today," Detective Stevenson said as she and Detective Williams entered the interrogation room and sat down.

"It's our pleasure. Andrea was our best friend. We would do anything to help you all find out who murdered her," Veronica said.

"Thank you. I'm Detective Williams, this is Detective Stevenson. Can you ladies start by telling us how you know Andrea?"

"Yeah, so I met Andrea when we worked at Walmart together. She was super nice and really pretty. She was fun and easy to talk to. We became fast friends. We started talking and she confided in me and told me how she was a foster kid, her mom was on drugs, and her grandma had died. She told me she was turning 18 soon and needed a place to stay. She told me she wouldn't be able to stay with her foster mom anymore, so I told her she could move in with me. I was 21, and I had my own place, I told her we could be roommates. So she said it sounded like a good plan to her," Veronica said.

"Then I moved in when Andrea moved in. I was a foster kid too," Riley said. "We met because we went to high school together. We were seeing a counselor at school, and they thought we would get along since we were both foster kids. At first I thought I wasn't going to like Andrea. She was pretty, a lot of guys liked her, and I thought she would be stuck up. But she turned out to be cool, and we became fast friends too. I needed to move out of my foster home as well. Not because I was turning 18, though. I was still 17 when I moved out," Riley said.

"So why did you need to move out?" Detective Stevenson asked.

"My foster parents were only in it for the money." Riley began to say. "They were neglectful and abusive. I didn't have any siblings so I just left. One of my counselors told me that I could get emancipated, but that I would need a roof over my head if I was going to do that. It worked out in my favor because my foster parents didn't even notice I was gone when I left to go stay with Dre and V. So I told Dre that I didn't want to stay in my foster home anymore and that I was trying to get emancipated. I told her I needed a place to stay, and that's when she told me she was moving in with Veronica. I was thinking of moving with my boyfriend at the time. He was 19 and staying with some of his friends, but I didn't want to be there either. Dre introduced me to Veronica, and I decided to stay with them."

"Yeah, and I was fine with having another roommate," Veronica said. "We could split the rent three ways instead of two, and still have some left over money. And Riley was cool. We all got along, and had a little Golden Girls moment. Except Riley was Latina and I'm Black, it's only three of us, and we ain't old."

"That's great that you all got along like that. So Riley, Veronica and Andrea worked at Walmart. Did you work there as well?" Detective Stevenson asked.

"No, I worked at McDonald's," Riley responded. "I had been working there since I was fourteen. We all were making minimum wage. We had some leftover money because we split the rent and bills three ways, but we wanted more. We wanted nicer things, you know? And the money we were making from those minimum wage jobs wasn't enough."

"Yeah, and that's when I decided to become a sugar baby," Veronica chimed in. "One of my cousins told me about the app. My cousin was a sugar baby, and she was getting all these nice shoes and handbags and taking nice trips. She had a new car and place, and I wanted in. I uploaded a few pictures on the app and met my first sugar daddy. He was a 58-year-old business owner here in Chicago. I started spending time with him, got some money, and got fired from my job at Walmart. So I was able to get unemployment for a while, and money from my sugar daddy. Being a sugar baby paid so well, I decided to make it a full-time job."

"So how long were you a sugar baby before you told Riley and Andrea about it?" Detective Williams asked.

"I had been doing it for a month," Veronica began. "The first two weeks, I would meet up with my sugar daddy and still do my shift at Walmart. But then he told me that I didn't have to work anymore, and that was all I needed to hear. So I missed the next two weeks of work. I told Dre and Ri I was going on a trip to Vegas with my sugar daddy. I sent them pictures because I wanted them to know where I was and what was going on just in case something happened to me. Something like what happened to Dre." Veronica looked down and began to cry when she said this last part. "I… I picked up some clothes for Dre and Ri while I was in Vegas. I had to bring my girls back some gifts, all on my sugar daddy. When I came back home, I brought them back some shoes and a dress so we could go out partying. Dre and Riley were really happy."

"Yeah, we thought it was sweet of Veronica to think of us while she was away," Riley said, through her tears. "She told us she had a good time. That her sugar daddy was nice to her, spoiled her, and treated her like a princess. She said he treated her better than any man had ever treated her before. So, Dre and I thought that this sounded better than working at Walmart and McDonald's so we asked Veronica about the app. We signed up and put some pictures up, and both of us had sugar daddies the next day."

"So are you all still sugar babies?" Detective Stevenson asked.

"Yeah," both girls responded.

"Even after what happened to Andrea?" Detective Williams asked.

"Listen, Detectives, I know it may sound stupid, especially after what happened to Dre, but we've gotten used to this lifestyle. We can't let it go that easily," Veronica said.

"I understand. Emily told us that you all would share creepy sugar daddy stories with each other. Tell us about that?" Detective Stevenson asked.

"We would just talk about some of the cringey and kinky stuff the sugar daddies were into, but nothing we ever shared seemed murderish," Riley began to cry even more now.

"Andrea never shared anything alarming with us, except for two things," Veronica said. "The first was when Albert Little, her third sugar daddy, told her that he wanted her to break up with Calvin and Nicholas or else. I told her she should break up with them if Albert was willing to take care of her, but Andrea never wanted anything serious and she was always worried about Emily."

"Veronica told Andrea to just stay with Albert since he really wanted to be with her. Veronica is engaged to her second sugar daddy now," Riley said.

"If you felt like she should do what he said, why did you think it was alarming, Veronica?" Detective Williams asked.

"Because Andrea got a third sugar daddy because Nicholas and Calvin couldn't devote as much time and money to her that she needed. Both of them had multiple girlfriends. Nicholas had a wife and kids, and Calvin had a consistent girlfriend. I told Andrea it would never work with them, and instead of worrying about getting money from them, she could just be with Albert, and he would take care of her. But that's not what she wanted," Veronica explained.

"So you both knew that Calvin and Nicholas had multiple girlfriends too?" Detective Stevenson asked.

"Yeah, Nicholas was a serial cheater when it came to his wife. And Calvin was a fine doctor who could get any woman he wanted. Andrea knew that she would always have to share them, but she was okay with that because that meant they didn't have to be serious," Riley said.

"She didn't like that Albert was so sensitive and wanted things to be serious," Veronica began. "That wasn't Andrea's speed. She was just in it for the money, not for love. I started out that way, but I ended up meeting a man that I love and getting engaged. I told her that she could do the same. I get it, that's not what Andrea wanted, but Andrea didn't realize that those other women who were with Nicholas and Calvin would get jealous. And what's that saying? You know, the one about a woman being scorned?"

"Hell hath no fury like a woman scorned," Detective Stevenson answered, and as she did she thought about Emily. These were the same words Emily had quoted when they first talked about Andrea's murder.

"Veronica, you said there were two things that were alarming when it came to Andrea. You mentioned Albert's threat as the first thing. What was the second thing?" Detective Williams asked.

"Right, so Albert's threat was only alarming to me because I felt that he would cut Andrea off completely, and she would have to depend on Nicholas and Calvin and look for another sugar daddy as well. That was the only thing with Albert. It had nothing to do with Andrea coming up murdered. But this…" Veronica pulled out her phone and went to her voicemail messages. "When you press play, you'll hear the voice of a woman threatening Andrea. This was a voicemail message that Andrea received and then sent to me six weeks ago."

"And that's not the only one. The woman sent ten more after that one. All over a three week span," Riley said.

"Emily told us that when you found Andrea's body, she had been dead for almost two weeks," Veronica said. "So we think the woman sent these messages to Andrea right before she killed her or had someone to kill her. In all the messages, she mentions Nicholas Wright."

"So the woman, she was one of Nicholas Wright's girlfriends?" Detective Williams asked.

"Yeah, and we could tell it wasn't his wife because this woman sounds young. We know that his wife was an older woman. Andrea told us, and we saw pictures of them on social media," Riley said.

"We think that this is the woman who murdered Andrea, and we think that's why they took her phone when they murdered her,"

Veronica said. "They knew that they sent these threatening voicemails to her. Little did they know I told my girl to send those messages to me just in case something were to ever happen to her."

"Why didn't you girls bring this in?" Detective Stevenson asked.

"Once we saw it on the news, we wanted to contact Emily first," Riley said. "We went over Mama Kim's house to talk to Emily, but she wasn't there. Mama Kim said Emily told her she was staying with a friend. Then Emily reached out to us the next day and told us that the murderer had Andrea's phone and had been texting her. That's when we told Emily that we could come by the police station or y'all could come to where we are to let you hear this. Emily told us not to come or share our evidence yet because you were busy talking to the sugar daddies and their wives."

"You all didn't tell Emily about the voicemails?" Detective Stevenson asked.

"No, Andrea didn't want Emily to know about the voicemails," Riley began saying as Veronica shook her head. "She knew Emily would be worried, and she didn't want her to worry about her. We didn't want to tell Emily over the phone because we thought it would be better for her to hear it with the cops so they could handle it."

"Yeah, Emily is our girl too," Veronica said, though her tears. "Andrea cared about her way too much, so we care about her too. We didn't want anything to happen to her. We thought if she heard the messages she may try to find the person, and that could put her in danger. We already lost Dre, we didn't want to lose Emily too."

"Okay, thank you both for this. This could really help us," Detective Stevenson said.

"Like we said, anything to find Dre's murderer," Riley replied.

"You want me to press play now?" Veronica asked.

"Yes, go ahead, play all of them," Detective Stevenson said.

Veronica pressed the play button on her phone. The detectives heard the first voicemail. On the voicemail, you could hear the voice of a woman threatening Andrea. They told her that she had better leave Nicholas alone, or they would kill her. They knew what kind of car she drove and they knew how she looked. That voicemail ended.

"Do you want me to play the next one?" Veronica asked.

"Yeah, but before you do, did Andrea ever tell Nicholas about this?" Detective Stevenson asked.

"Yeah, because he failed to mention it during his interrogation," Detective Williams said.

“Andrea felt like it wasn’t a big deal,” Veronica responded. “She actually laughed about it. But she did wonder how the girl got her number. So she said she told Nicholas that one of his girlfriends was leaving threatening voicemails on her phone. He apologized and said that they must’ve looked at his phone while he was asleep or in the shower or something. She never played the voicemails for him.”

“Alright, play the next one,” Detective Stevenson said. Veronica played the next voicemail. This time, they heard a child crying in the background. “The woman has a kid?”

“That’s what we thought,” Riley said.

“You think Nicholas Wright has an illegitimate kid?” Detective Williams asked.

“I don’t know, but that voice does sound familiar to me,” Detective Stevenson said. “Play another one.”

Veronica played another voicemail. Detective Stevenson still couldn’t make out the voice, but she knew the voice sounded familiar to her. This time, the child in the background said a name faintly. “Wait, play that again, the kid said a name.”

“It sounded like he just said mama,” Detective Williams said.

"No, it was a name. Play it again." Veronica played the voicemail again, but Detective Stevenson still couldn't make out the name the child said. "Veronica, can I borrow your phone for a second? I need to have one of my guys play this slowly so I can hear the kid in the background."

"Yeah, go ahead." Detective Stevenson grabbed Veronica's phone and walked out of the interrogation room.

"Stevenson, he said mama, he didn't say a name I heard him," Detective Williams stood up and followed her out. Detective Stevenson walked to another officer's desk while Detective Williams was chasing after her.

"Flores, hook this up to your computer. Play it slow. There is a child saying something in the background, a name. I can't make it out." After that, the chief, Emily, Detective Williams, Veronica, and Riley all crowded in around her.

"Stevie," Detective Williams called Detective Stevenson, but she shushed him. Officer Flores plugged the phone into his computer. He slowed down the voicemail. The child said the name, but Detective Stevenson still couldn't hear it.

"Play it louder, Flores, and keep playing it slow." Officer Flores turned up the volume on the voicemail again and slowed it down. Detective Stevenson finally heard the name the child was saying in the background, and by hearing the name, she finally recognized the voice.

"I knew it! I knew that I knew that voice. Williams, let's go, I know where that person is. Chief, I'll need backup. I need about four police cars with two officers in each," Detective Stevenson grabbed her coat and headed out the door.

"YOU HEARD HER, MOVE OUT!" the chief yelled. Eight officers and Detective Williams all followed Detective Stevenson out the door.

"Emily, do you know who it was?" Veronica asked.

"No, I don't know, but I trust Detective Stevenson. If she says she knows, she knows."

Part 5 : The Confession

Chapter 8 - "Hell Hath No Fury Like a Woman Scorned"

Detective Stevenson, Detective Williams, and the four police vehicles surrounded the house where Andrea's murderer should be. There were officers in the back and front of the house. There were officers up the street and down the street. The detectives walked up to the door to knock on it.

"Are you sure about this, Stevie?" Detective Williams asked.

"Yes, I'm positive." Detective Stevenson knocked on the door. "This is Detective Stevenson and Detective Williams, open up." A young woman opened the door afterward.

"Is everything okay, Detectives?" the young woman asked.

"We're looking for Mrs. Wright," Detective Williams said as he and Detective Stevenson stood at the front door of Nicholas and Amber Wright's house.

"She's upstairs, I'm her assistant. Come in, I'll call her down." Amber Wright's assistant opened the door and the detectives came into the Wright's home.

"Detectives, you're back. To what do I owe the pleasure? Is Nicholas in more trouble?" Amber Wright asked after her assistant asked her to come downstairs.

"Not him this time," Detective Williams said.

"Well, who? Me?" Amber Wright asked. "We went over this Detective, I had nothing to do with that girl's murder."

"Where is your nanny?" Detective Stevenson asked.

"Dana? What does she have to do with anything?"

"We believe that she is the one who murdered Andrea Kane," Detective Stevenson said.

“Don’t be absurd. Why would Dana murder that girl?” Mrs. Wright asked.

“Because Dana was in love with Nicholas Wright,” Detective Stevenson said. “We have a voicemail recording of Dana threatening Andrea Kane, and in the background we heard one of your children saying her name.”

“And whoever killed Andrea had her phone and her keys,” Detective Williams said. “They’ve been texting Andrea’s sister from the phone. They told the sister that they killed her because she was sleeping with the man they loved.”

“It all makes sense why Andrea’s body was found at Nicholas’ construction site,” Detective Stevenson added.

“Did you know that Nicholas and Dana had been together?” Detective Williams asked.

“No, and I don’t care, she's been taking care of my children and she’s out with them right now, ” Amber Wright said, frantically. “I’ve had a killer taking care of my children.”

“I don’t think she’ll hurt your children Mrs. Wright…” Detective Stevenson began.

“YOU DON’T KNOW THAT,” Mrs. Wright said hysterically.

"Where is Dana?" Detective Williams asked, rubbing Amber Wright's arm trying to calm her down.

"She's not here right now, she took the kids to the park a couple blocks away," Mrs. Wright said. "Do you want to wait here for her? She'll be back soon."

"No, I'll tell our officers to lay low. Detective Williams and I will go to the park and find Dana. Mrs. Wright, you may want to come with us so you can get your children."

"What about my children? They'll be traumatized seeing their nanny get arrested."

"Don't worry, we'll get them to walk back home with you before the arrest happens."

The detectives walked to the park. They didn't want Dana seeing their car or any police cars. Once they got to the park, they saw Nicholas and Amber Wright's children playing. Dana was sitting on a bench with a cell phone in her hands. Detective Stevenson walked over to sit on the side of Dana, while Detective Williams sat a few benches down.

"Hi Dana," Detective Stevenson said as she sat next to Dana. She could tell Dana was startled when she sat down next to her and said hello. Dana put the phone that was in her hands away in her bag. It was at this moment that Detective Stevenson knew that the phone Dana was holding belonged to Andrea Kane.

"Hi, Detective Stevenson. What are you doing here?" Dana asked nervously.

"Oh, I just had some more questions about the case. You didn't text me back about your conversations with Mrs. Wright?"

"Oh, yeah, that. Well, Amber got drunk and said she wanted Nicholas to get rid of Andrea. People started finding out that she was a sugar baby, and it made them look bad as a couple. I think he might have hired someone to take Andrea out, but it was only because Amber wanted him too. He'll do anything she wants him to," Dana responded.

"Is that so?" Detective Stevenson asked.

"Yes, she told me a couple nights ago. I was busy with some things so I forgot to tell you. She even mentioned Nicholas has sent his hit men to scare some of his workers. I was thinking maybe Nicholas told the workers not to tell about what happened to the girl."

"Well Dana, it's funny you mention that. My partner and I have reason to believe that Andrea Kane's killer was a woman and that, possibly, a man transported her body to the construction site." Dana stared at Detective Stevenson, quietly.

"What…what makes you think that?" Dana asked.

"Well, we think that one of Nicholas' girlfriends became jealous of Andrea. You know, jealous of her beauty, Nicholas' attraction to her, and of him supporting her. We think that this jealous girlfriend felt like Andrea was in the way of their relationship with Nicholas. Maybe they felt that they would never be able to fully get Nicholas' attention with Andrea in the way, so they killed her, shot her four times, froze her body, and transported her to Nicholas' construction site. Her body stayed frozen because this girlfriend knew that Nicholas' construction crew couldn't work for two weeks because of his legal issues. They knew that Andrea's body would sit there day after day, freezing. And we believe that this girlfriend knew that, eventually, Andrea's body would be found and Nicholas would see that his beautiful sugar baby was dead. In an act of jealous rage, one of his girlfriends murdered Andrea. I assume they wanted Nicholas to see how serious they were about their relationship with him. They wanted Nicholas to see how much they longed for *all* of his attention."

Detective Stevenson scooted closer to Dana. "Now Dana, we can do this the easy way or the hard way."

Once Detective Stevenson finished talking, Dana quickly stood up to run across the park. She ran about seven feet and was stopped and grabbed by Detective Williams. He tackled Dana to the ground and handcuffed her. All while Detective Stevenson was talking, Dana hadn't noticed Detective Williams in the distance. Neither did she notice Amber Wright walking home with her children. Detective Williams lifted Dana off the ground and placed her in a squad car. Once Dana was placed in the squad car with the door closed the detectives looked at one another.

"Great work, Stevie," Detective Williams said.

"You too. Let's get back to the station and get her to talk."

"Well we know she killed Andrea, we just need her to confess."

"Yeah, but like we've been saying, Dana didn't move Andrea's dead body by herself. Nor did she freeze it herself. She's too small and too young. Dana had to have an accomplice and we don't know who that is yet."

The detectives drove back to the police station. Dana was placed in an interrogation room. Emily, Veronica, and Riley both stood up when Dana was brought into the police station. As Dana was escorted to the interrogation room by the police, Emily saw her face. After seeing Dana's face, Emily realized this was the woman who killed her sister, left the voicemails, and sent her the text messages pretending to be Andrea. It was her — she was finally here. As she stood staring at Dana, tears welling in her eyes, Detective Stevenson walked up to Emily and placed her hand on her shoulder.

"That's her. We got her. Do you want to go behind the window with the chief?"

"Yeah…yeah, I'm ready," Emily wiped her eyes. She and the chief walked behind the interrogation room window. Emily stared at Dana and felt conflicted. Dana looked to only be a couple years older than Andrea, and in Dana's eyes, Emily saw herself. She saw a helpless young girl who was scared. In Dana's eyes, she saw Andrea too, a young girl who was confused and trying to figure things out. She pitied Dana but hated her at the same time. Emily was at a loss for words; everything around her seemed to fade away, and all she saw was Dana. The detectives walked into the interrogation room where Dana was handcuffed.

“Hands on the table,” Detective Williams said aggressively, as he and Detective Stevenson sat down across from Dana. He placed Andrea’s keys and her phone, which were confiscated from Dana’s bag, on the table. “These yours?”

Dana hung her head down and began to cry. She shook her head no.

“Are these Andrea’s keys and phone?” Detective Stevenson asked, and Dana nodded her head yes. “Have you been using this phone to text Andrea’s sister, Emily, pretending that you were Andrea?” Dana sat still, crying, and didn’t respond. “ANSWER ME!” Detective Stevenson said as she banged her hand on the table. Dana was frightened by the bang and jumped in her seat, but through her crying, she responded yes.

“Dana, why did you do it?” Detective Williams asked.

“Yeah, tell us. We’re dying to know,” Detective Stevenson said, but Dana just sat crying. “Okay, I see we’re going to have to take the long road to a confession with you. Alright then, tell us when and how you fell in love with Nicholas Wright.”

For a moment, Dana just sat there. Then she asked, “Is this being recorded?”

"Yes, on that camera up there. Why?" Detective Stevenson asked.

"Because I want you to promise me that you'll show Nicholas the video. I never really told him how I felt," Dana said and the detectives looked at one another in shock by Dana's comment.

"We can't make that promise until you give us a confession," Detective Stevenson prodded, frowning.

"Okay, I'll confess." Dana lifted her head and said, "I killed her. I killed Andrea Kane."

"Okay, now tell us why and how you did it. We promise we'll show the recording to Nicholas," Detective Stevenson said, while Dana sat crying.

"I became a nanny for the Wrights a couple years ago. I interviewed with Mrs. Wright, and she told me they'd had many nannies come and go. She hoped I would be the one to stay. I asked her if she was single. She told me that her husband would be there from time to time, but for the most part, only she and the kids would be home. I saw how nice their house was and how nicely dressed Amber Wright was. I admired her. She told me that she and her husband co-own the number one construction company in Chicago. I was honored to be their nanny. I had never worked for people with so much money and status, and with such a wonderful home. I was hired, and after a couple of weeks on the job, I finally met Nicholas. I saw that anytime he would come around Amber was furious with him. They were always arguing about something. If it wasn't the business, it was about his cheating or her cheating. If it wasn't that, it was the kids. If it wasn't the kids, it was her dad. I started noticing why so many nannies had left before. I was on the verge of leaving myself." Dana wiped her nose with her sleeve.

"Why didn't you?" Detective Stevenson asked.

"One day, I spent the day with Nicholas and the kids. They spent the day with him when Mrs. Wright had some business to take care of. He was such a great father. He was a terrific cook. He made all of the kids' meals. He was nice to me and asked me a lot of questions about myself. After spending the day with him and the kids, I left that night and came back the next morning. The kids spent the rest of the day with Nicholas and then went back home with Mrs. Wright because they had school the next day. I spent the rest of the day with Mrs. Wright, and came back the next morning to get the kids ready for school. After the kids went to school, Mrs. Wright went to the gym. Nicholas texted me and told me that their daughter, Maddie, forgot her stuffed animal. He told me that I could come over and get it. I went back over to his house. I grabbed the stuffed animal, and Nicholas asked me if I would like to stay for coffee. I stayed, we had coffee, and then one thing led to another and we slept together. I was upset with myself for doing that with Nicholas."

"Why?" Detective Williams said.

"Because of Mrs. Wright. I felt like I had betrayed her. But Nicholas told me that they were no longer together. They were free to see other people, and they were only together for their kids. He told me that Mrs. Wright wasn't just going to the gym to workout, and that she had been seeing her trainer. I didn't know if this was true or not. So when I went back to Mrs. Wright's house, I asked her if she had a good time at the gym. She told me that she had a great time. She seemed to be drunk. She poured a glass of wine for herself and asked me if I wanted a glass. I didn't want to say yes, but she poured me a glass anyway. She told me I wouldn't get fired for drinking with her, and that the kids weren't back home yet. After we drank a bit, she told me that she was seeing her trainer. I asked her if Nicholas knew about this. She waved her hand and told me yes, that they have an open relationship. She said that he sleeps with who he wants, and she sleeps with who she wants, and that's just the way their marriage is. I didn't tell her about me and Nicholas. I figured that since they had an open marriage, it wasn't a big deal."

"So how and when did you find out about Andrea?" Detective Williams asked.

"I was over Nicholas' house one day. This was after five months of me working. He was in the shower. A message popped up on his phone. I saw that it was from a contact named 'sugar baby'. I knew his passcode because I had seen him put it in before. I looked at the message and looked at the timeline of messages. I saw that they had been having a relationship for a while. I saw messages where he had sent her money, where they went out to dinner together, everything. She was beautiful, and I just got so upset and jealous. I was upset because I loved Nicholas, and he had never taken me out to dinner or bought me anything. I confronted him about it. I asked him who Andrea Kane was. He told me she was his sugar baby. He told me that they spent time together, he took her to parties, and he bought her nice things for spending time with him. She was a beautiful young woman that he could have on his arm. I asked him why he never did any of those things for me or with me. He said…" Dana paused.

"He said what?" Detective Stevenson asked.

"He said it was because I wasn't his sugar baby, I was his children's nanny. He said I was a beautiful girl, but I wasn't Andrea. He said that buying her gifts and taking her to nice places was a part of the deal. Our deal was sleeping together and keeping it from Mrs. Wright. I was upset about what he said, but I never told Nicholas that what he said hurt. I never stopped being with him. Then I started stalking Andrea's social media. I saw how she got nice shoes and handbags, and she went to nice places. Then I saw Nicholas' messages again, and he asked her to go to Vegas with him, and she said yes. The whole time he was out of town, I was with Mrs. Wright and the kids. I became so upset. I wanted to take Andrea's place — I wanted to have Nicholas' attention and get treated well like her. That's when I knew I had to get rid of her." Dana wasn't crying anymore, she was angry.

"So how did you do it?" Detective Williams asked.

"One day, I saw that he told Andrea that he loved her. He had never told me that he loved me. So that's when I really wanted to get rid of her. I started texting her from Nicholas' phone whenever I would go over to be with him. I started getting to know her and asking her how she was. I had played it over and over in my mind that I would tell her to leave Nicholas alone or I would kill her. I started threatening her by leaving her voicemails. Then one day I saw that she asked Nicholas if he wanted to spend time together. He told her he couldn't because his son had a volleyball game. I decided that this would be the day I would do it. When the family was ready to go to the game I hid Nicholas' phone and said that Maddie must've hidden it. I told them that I would stay and find it. I texted Andrea, pretending to be Nicholas, and told her I would spend time with her. I told her that the game was canceled because of the coronavirus. I texted her an address where to meet me, and she told me that she would Uber there. She told me that she was downtown grabbing some Starbucks and shopping a bit, but she would be on her way."

"Then what happened? What was the address you texted her?" Detective Stevenson asked.

"You might as well tell us. We have the phone right here, we can easily look it up," Detective Williams said.

"I told her to meet me at a cabin in LaSalle county. The cabin is my brother's Airbnb. The cabin is on 25 acres of land. She came all the way out there just to be with Nicholas."

“So was it your brother who helped you freeze and move her body?” Detective Williams asked.

“No, my brother lives in Chicago. He has an employee of his who stays on the 25 acres and cleans the cabin. His name is Danny Monker. He did some time in prison for attempted murder. He kills deer and stuff, so I knew he would be fine with helping me if it got to the point where I needed to kill Andrea. Andrea drove out to the cabin. I was waiting for her inside. She asked Nicholas where his car was. I pretended to be him and told her I was inside, and that I had taken an Uber to the cabin. When she walked in, I gave her my stipulations. I was holding Danny’s shotgun as I told her that she had to promise to stay away from Nicholas, or else. She said she would stay away. I put the gun down, and told her to go. But… she didn’t leave. She walked out the door, and I walked out after. I set the gun down by the door, and she started to fight me once I set the gun down. We fought for a while. We hit each other with objects, all of that. Finally I was able to get to the gun, and I shot her four times. There was blood everywhere. Danny heard the shots and came running to the cabin. He asked me what I had done. I didn’t say anything because I didn’t mean to kill her. Then Danny said he was going to call the police, and I told him that if he did he'd be in trouble too. I told him that he was a convicted felon, and that he had better help me or else I would tell my brother and the cops that he did it. I mean who were they going to believe, me or him? I told him that I would kill him too since I was holding the shotgun."

"So then what happened?" Detective Williams asked.

"Then we needed to move her body. I took her phone, purse, and keys. We placed her in a garbage bag and placed her in a freezer in the basement that Danny used for his animal meat when he hunted. We kept her there for a couple of hours. I knew the Wright's would be back home so we had to move her. I knew I would have to hurry back and clean myself before the Wright's came back. Danny asked me if I wanted to keep her on the property. I told him no, I knew exactly where to place her. So we put her body in a black garbage bag in the back of his pickup truck. It was cold out, and his pick-up truck was covered in snow. So her body was still cold. Danny put snow on top of her body as well. He drove me back to my apartment to get cleaned up, then he drove her dead body to the construction site. No one was there. He was able to sneak in easily because the construction site is next to an alley. He threw her body over the gate at the construction site and then jumped the gate. He placed her body in a certain spot and covered it with the bags of cement mix. It was January, so it got dark around 6:00. So it was already dark by the time he did it.

"I knew the Wrights would be coming back home by 8:00, so I took a shower and changed clothes, and then Danny picked me up from my apartment and dropped me off at the Wrights' house. I knew the Wrights wouldn't notice what I was wearing and that I had changed clothes. I was back just in time for them to come home with Nicholas' phone. I pretended that I found the phone. I deleted all of the messages I sent to Andrea, and I kept her phone instead. I felt bad about killing her, but I felt that now I could finally have Nicholas to myself. He and I spent some time together in those two weeks before Andrea was found dead. It was great because there were no calls from her, he wasn't planning to spend time with her, and the icing on the cake was I pretended that she ghosted him so he wouldn't want to see her again."

"Did it work?" Detective Stevenson asked.

"No, he still missed her. Anyway, because of the legal issues he was having with his construction company, I knew he wouldn't be in trouble even if everything was connected back to him. He also was at his son's volleyball game, so he wasn't around her at all that day. The last thing I needed to get rid of was Andrea's sister. Since I had the keys, I tried going by the address that was listed on her I.D., but when I went by the keys didn't work for the building. So I pretended to be Andrea so her sister didn't get worried. I wanted Nicholas to find her dead. I wanted him to talk to me about it so I could tell him how serious I was about us being together. But you two arrested Mrs. Wright as well. I thought Nicholas would talk to me about it, but he didn't. He talked to Mrs. Wright about it. And then he seemed to be mourning Andrea's passing. Even after she was dead, this girl was coming between Nicholas and I. He hasn't really talked to me since he found out. I just wanted this to be recorded because I want him to know how much I love him," The detectives sat looking at Dana astonished, after she said this part. They had come in contact with many delusional killers in the past, but she said so many things that they weren't expecting.

"Well Dana, looks like you'll be spending life in prison for the death of Andrea Kane. Williams let's go get Danny," Detective Stevenson said as a police officer came in to take Dana away.

Emily, the chief, Veronica, and Riley came out from behind the window. Emily hugged the two detectives, crying.

“Thank you,” Emily said as she hugged them.

“Don’t thank us just yet, we have one more person to arrest,” Detective Stevenson said as she and Detective Williams headed for their squad car with the other police officers in tow. They drove to the cabin in LaSalle County. They told the police officers to keep their cars back. They were on 25 acres of land and didn’t want Danny to run anywhere. As they all surrounded the house, Detective Williams knocked on the door and announced that they were there, no one opened the door. One of the officers kicked in the door and saw that all the lights were off, the curtains were closed, and it was completely dark inside the cabin. The detectives moved in slowly, shining their flashlights and pointing their guns. As they kept walking they motioned towards the officers to come in. As the other officers came in, Danny fired his shotgun. The officers and detectives ducked down. Danny was at the top of the stairs shooting at the officers and detectives. When the officers who were standing behind the house came in through the back door, Danny tried climbing out of a window at the top of the stairs. He jumped down from the window, but the police officers standing by told him to drop his weapon. Danny shot at them. He shot both officers in the arm and began running toward his pickup truck that was eight feet away. Detective Williams and Detective Stevenson came out from behind his pickup truck with their guns pointed at Danny.

"Stop," Detective Stevenson yelled, but Danny kept running towards them, still firing. Then Detective Williams shot at Danny once. When he missed, Detective Stevenson shot at Danny twice. One bullet hit him in the arm and the other in the leg. Danny fell to the ground. His gun fell with him. After seeing Danny down on the ground, the detectives ran over to him. Danny began to reach for his gun again upon seeing them come closer to him

"Don't even think about it," Detective Stevenson said as she and Detective Williams stood over Danny with their guns pointed at him. Danny moved his hand away from the gun. Detective Stevenson picked up the gun as Detective Williams handcuffed Danny. Danny was handcuffed and driven away in an ambulance so they could treat his wounds. Officers rode in the ambulance with Danny and drove behind the ambulance.

“Alright Stevie, let’s go tell Emily we got him,” Detective Williams said, putting his hand on Detective Stevenson’s shoulder.

The detectives drove back to the police station with a big weight lifted off of their shoulders. It was 5:00 pm on February 13th. Detective Williams and Detective Stevenson were overjoyed to have found Andrea Kane’s killers in just four days. This was a new record for them and as they walked back into the police station, all of the police officers, the chief, Emily, Riley, and Veronica all stood up to give them a round of applause. The detectives walked over to Emily, who hugged them both again, crying.

“Thank you. Thank you for caring enough about Andrea to find them.”

“Emily, we couldn’t have done it without you,” Detective Williams replied, grinning.

“Yes, it was because of your courage, your smarts, and your cooperation that we were able to find them so quickly,” Detective Stevenson said as they both started to clap for Emily, and everyone else at the police station did as well. Emily was in awe of the applause and blushed as they all applauded her.

"Can you drive me over to Mama Kim's house? I have to tell her," Emily asked as Veronica and Riley hugged her.

"Sure, let's go," Detective Stevenson said.

"Well, I'm going to stop by the store and get my wife a gift. Tomorrow is Valentine's Day," Detective Williams said.

"It is, that's right. I almost forgot," Detective Stevenson said.

"You wanna double date with us, Stevie? Since you got a man and all?"

"I'll let you know."

"Good, because I'm dying to meet him. Alright you ladies, take care of Ms. Baker."

"We will," Veronica said. "Emily, we'll come with you to tell Mama Kim."

"Okay, let's go." Detective Stevenson followed behind Andrea and Veronica's car as they drove to Ms. Kimberly Baker's house. Once they were there, Detective Stevenson sat outside to watch Emily, Veronica, and Riley tell Ms. Kimberly Baker the great news. As she watched, she noticed Ms. Kimberly Baker started to cry, and the girls all started to hug her and cry as well. Seeing all of these emotions brought tears to Detective Stevenson's own eyes and joy to her heart.

Through her dashboard window, she saw Emily pointing at her car. Ms. Kimberly Baker started walking down her porch stairs towards Detective Stevenson's car. She exited the car so Ms. Kimberly Baker could hug her as well.

"Thank you for helping my girls, thank you for putting Andrea at peace," Ms. Kimberly Baker said as she hugged Detective Stevenson and cried on her shoulder.

"It was no problem, ma'am, just doing my job."

"No, you did more than your job. You cared. Emily told me about how you didn't rest until you found Andrea's killer. How you let her stay with you, how you clothed her and everything. Thank you."

"You're welcome, Ms. Baker."

"All of my babies call me Mama Kim. Please call me Mama Kim." Ms. Kimberly Baker looked Detective Stevenson in the eyes and smiled.

"You're welcome, Mama Kim." Detective Stevenson grinned as tears filled her eyes. "So what are you all going to do about Andrea? Are you going to have a funeral or a memorial?"

"Well Emily, what would you like to do?" Ms. Kimberly Baker asked.

“I think we should cremate Andrea. That way all of us can keep some of her ashes,” Emily said. “Our grandma was cremated as well, so Andrea wouldn’t be buried next to anybody. I think she’d be lonely at some cemetery by herself.”

“Well, I’ll leave you all to start making arrangements for that. Let me know if you need anything.” Detective Stevenson started to get back in her car, but Emily ran down from the porch to say one last thing to Detective Stevenson before she left.

“Wait, Detective Stevenson, do you want to come in?” Emily asked. “I'm sure Mama Kim can cook something for us.”

“No, Emily, I actually have something I need to do.”

“Oh, you have another date?”

“No, I’m…I’m going to go home and call my family,” Detective Stevenson said, and Emily looked surprised. “I know. It’s been a while, but I decided to take your advice. It hasn’t steered me wrong this far.”

“That’s great, Detective Stevenson, I have some exciting news too.”

“Well, besides helping us find your sister’s murderer, what?”

“Well, I was talking to the chief. You know, all those times you and Detective Williams left me at the station and when he and I were behind the window. I asked him what I’d have to do to become a police officer. He told me what the process entails, and I think I’m going to drop out of school and join the police academy.”

“Emily, are you sure you want to do that? I thought you wanted to be a psychologist?”

“Well, I’ll still get to apply my background in psychology when I become a detective. And who knows, maybe I’ll get a Ph.D. like Detective Williams. I really want to do this. You all have inspired me. I want to help people like you two do. Without you two, we wouldn’t have ever found who murdered my sister. Thanks for listening to me and for caring about Andrea and I, because not a lot of people have.” Emily cried as Detective Stevenson hugged her. “We have a new mother now. You’re our mother who brought us peace.”

After hearing these words, Detective Stevenson began to cry as well. She hugged Emily so tight and for longer than she expected to at that moment. In this small amount of time, she had developed a love for Emily like she was her own daughter, and she was so proud that she wanted to follow in her footsteps and become a detective.

"I'm sorry to get you so emotional," Emily said.

"No, it's okay. I haven't cried in a while, you know."

"Okay, I'm going to let you go home so you can call your family."

"Okay." Detective Stevenson got back in her car and Emily went back on the porch with Ms. Kimberly Baker. Detective Stevenson kept crying as she drove home. She pondered what her father would say once she called him. She wondered if he would be upset with her for not calling him for so many years.

Ring. Ring. Ring.

"Hello," Detective Stevenson answered the phone.

"Hey Stevie, the chief is going to go to the media in an hour and let them know that we've found Andrea Kane's killer," Detective Williams explained on the other end.

"That's great," Detective Stevenson responded.

"Did Emily tell you what she wanted to do as far as funeral arrangements?"

"Yeah, she said she wants Andrea cremated. Their grandmother was cremated as well. And Emily, Ms. Baker, Veronica, and Riley will share the ashes."

"Okay, I'll let Coroner Burgess know."

"Willie," Detective Stevenson said, and Detective Williams just looked at the phone in disbelief. "Hello?"

"Oh you must be in a great mood, you never call me Willie unless you are."

"Shut up, I got great news. Emily wants to become a police officer so she can become a detective like us. She said we inspire her."

"Look at that, two Black cops inspiring a lil' White girl who's a foster kid to become a cop. I'll take it," Detective Williams laughed.

"Shut up, Williams." Detective Stevenson rolled her eyes and shook her head.

"Hey, you going to see your man?"

"No, I'm actually about to call home and talk to my dad and grandad."

"Whoa, okay. Let me know how that goes tomorrow?"

"I will. Bye Willie."

"Bye Stevie."

Detective Stevenson finally arrived home. She was procrastinating because she wasn't excited to call her father and grandfather. She turned on the television to see the chief give his announcement to the media about Andrea's death. They showed Dana and Danny on the news. They talked about her brother's Airbnb, and they talked about Emily Kane and her contribution to the case. Then the chief thanked both detectives who were a part of the case for their bravery, quick thinking, quick acting, and care for the case. Detective Stevenson was happy with the chief's speech. She completed some paperwork, and after a couple hours had passed, she finally gained enough courage to call home.

Ring. Ring. Ring.

"Hello," Detective Stevenson said, but no one responded on the other end. "Hello, is anyone there?"

"Is this my baby? Sarah?" Detective Stevenson's mother said on the other end of the phone as she began to cry. "Sarah?"

"Yeah Mom, it's me." Tears clouded Detective Stevenson's eyes.

"Sarah, it's so good to hear from you. We saw your case on the news, that you found the people who killed that poor girl," her mom said.

"You saw that?"

“Yes baby, we saw it. You did fantastic. I’m so glad you called. Your father and grandfather wanted to talk to you.”

“They did?”

“Yes, baby, they’re right here,” her mom said. “Harold, Winston, it’s Sarah.”

“Hello Sarah,” Detective Stevenson’s father said on the other end of the phone. She didn’t know what to say. She sat on her bed with the phone to her ear frozen. She hadn’t heard her father’s voice in years. “Sarah, are you still there?”

“Yeah…yeah, Dad, I’m still here.”

“Well, baby, you’re on speaker, so we’re all talking to you. Your grandpa is here too.”

“Oh, hey Grandpa Winston.”

“Hey Sarah, baby, I miss you. When are you coming home?” Grandpa Winston asked.

“Oh, I don’t know yet, Grandpa Winston.”

“Well, whenever you come, Sarah, we just wanted you to know we heard Chicago’s chief of police talking about the great work you did finding that girl’s murderer,” Detective Stevenson’s dad, Harold, said.

"Yeah, we just arrested them today," Detective Stevenson responded.

"Well, baby girl, I just wanted to let you know that we're all proud of you. What you did was fantastic. Finding that young lady's murderer so fast and bringing peace to her and her family. Great job," Harold said. When Detective Stevenson heard these words she began to cry. She had never heard her father tell her that he was proud of her for being a part of the police force. She held her mouth so her father wouldn't hear her cry. "Sarah, you still there?"

"Yeah Dad, uh…that's great to hear that from you. Thank you! Thank you for saying that," Detective Stevenson said, wiping her eyes.

"I know Grandpa Winston and I may have given you a lot of grief about becoming a police officer. It was only because we were worried about you being a Black woman and being a cop. We didn't want you to go through the same things we did or worse. You were our little girl and we wanted to protect you," Detective Stevenson's dad said.

"I know, Dad, it's fine."

"No, it's not fine. I know that's why you haven't really been back home since you left for Chicago. But I want you to come visit us more often. I’m retiring from the police force soon and your mother is throwing a party for me. She thinks it's a surprise, but I know all about it. I want you to come, it’ll be next week.”

“Yeah. Yeah Dad, I’ll…I’ll be there.”

“Sounds good. We love you Sarah, and keep doing the great work you do.”

“I love you all too. And thank you, I learned from the best. You and Grandpa Winston”

“Bye baby,” Harold said.

“Bye my baby, Sarah,” Detective Stevenson’s mom said.

“Bye grandbaby,” Grandpa Winston said.

“Bye you all, love you all.” Detective Stevenson hung up the phone. She felt so much tension and pain release from her body when she did this. Not only was talking to her dad and grandad the closure she needed, but hearing them say that they were proud of her also made her feel at ease. All this time, she didn’t realize how much she needed to hear her family say they were proud of her. She laid in bed crying and releasing all of the stress and happiness that Andrea Kane’s case brought her. After laying in bed crying for what seemed like an hour, but was actually only five minutes, her date called.

Ring. Ring. Ring.

"Hello."

Four days had passed since Dana and Danny were arrested for Andrea Kane's murder. It was now February 17th and it was the day of Andrea's memorial. Emily asked the chief to announce the date and time of the memorial on the local news so that anyone who wanted to come could pay their respects. The memorial was held at Ms. Kimberly Baker's church. Beautiful pictures of Andrea and beautiful flowers were placed all around her three urns that held her ashes. One urn was for her friends, Veronica and Riley, one urn was for Ms. Kimberly Baker, and one urn was for her sister, Emily. The priest stood and gave the eulogy for Andrea. In the crowd there were many different people. Emily, Veronica, Riley, and Ms. Kimberly Baker sat up front. Detective Williams along with his wife Cheryl and his twin boys sat behind them. Behind Detective Williams sat Nicholas Wright, Amber Wright, and their children. Behind the Wrights sat Calvin Bruno. Behind Calvin Bruno sat Albert Little. On the other side in the pews sat Lily Bostitch, and behind her sat Samantha Little. The chief of police sat in the back in the last pew. Many other people filled the church, scattered in different pews.

"Where is Detective Stevenson?" Emily asked Detective Williams.

"I don't know, she said she was on her way," Detective Williams responded. Afterwards, his phone vibrated.

Buzz. Buzz. Buzz.

"It's Stevie. She wants you to come outside, Emily," Emily stood up, looking confused, but headed outside.

When she came outside, she saw Detective Stevenson standing on the steps of the church.

"Detective Stevenson, what are you doing out here? Why don't you come in?"

"There is someone here that I want you to talk to," Detective Stevenson said. As she did she looked up the street to show Emily that her mother, Alexis, was standing up the street.

"You brought her here?" Emily asked.

"Yeah, I felt that you should talk to her. She may not want to come in, and you may not want her to come in, but I think you should talk to her," Detective Stevenson said.

"She didn't even believe me when I told her Andrea was dead. What should I say?"

"Well, I told her Andrea was dead, we caught her murderers, today is her memorial, and that she should come and see you. She told me that you wouldn't want to talk to her, but I told her that you did. Emily, your mother may be a drug addict, but she's still your mother. She put you through a lot of pain, but you all share the same pain as well. Just as you lost your grandmother, she lost her mother. Just as you lost your sister, she lost her daughter. Go talk to her."

"Okay." Emily walked down the stairs of the church and up the street to talk to her mother. She tapped her mother on the shoulder, and Alexis turned around. Neither one of them said anything to each other, and they just stared at each other for a moment. Alexis started to cry at that moment she realized Andrea was truly gone. Emily stood there hugging her mother and her mother hugged her.

"Emily, I, um…I just wanted to apologize to you. I didn't get to apologize to Dre, so I'm going to say this to you now. I'm sorry for being the mother I was, the mother I am. I'm sorry I didn't protect you and Dre. I'm sorry for leaving you all alone, and I'm sorry that Dre is gone. It's all my fault that she's gone," Alexis cried loudly.

"Mom, it's not your fault. Andrea was murdered, and that's why she's gone. And Detective Stevenson and Detective Williams arrested her murderers, who admitted to murdering her. They're going to be put away for a long time. Thank you for apologizing — you don't know how long I waited to hear that. How long I wanted to hear that. Do you want to come in? It's cold out."

"Yeah, yeah, I'll come in." Alexis and Emily began walking up the street towards the church where Detective Stevenson was still standing on the steps. Once they reached the doors, all three of them went into the church together. Once inside, Emily saw Calvin Bruno. This time she wasn't afraid to speak to him.

"Detective Stevenson, can you go sit with my mom at the front pew? I have someone that I need to talk to."

"Yeah, Emily. I can do that." Emily walked up to Calvin Bruno.

"Dr. Bruno?" Emily said.

"Emily, what are you doing…" Calvin Bruno began to say through his tears. Then he realized who Emily was. "Were you…?"

"I'm Andrea's little sister. I know she talked to you about me, and I've been around the entire time the detectives have been working on her case," Emily explained as Calvin Bruno stood up to apologize.

"Emily, I am so sorry. I didn't know..."

"I know you didn't know Andrea was my sister." Emily sat down next to Calvin as she beckoned him to sit back down. "I was upset with you at first for dating my sister. But I'm not anymore. She felt that you really cared about her."

"I did. She was a wonderful and beautiful person."

"Yeah, she was. Um...thank you for being a great professor. You taught me a lot about psychology. You were one of my favorite speakers. I just wanted to tell you that."

"Oh you're welcome, Emily." Calvin Bruno smiled. Then he looked down sadly. "I'm sure I let you down, by being your sister's sugar daddy."

"I can't hold that against you. You didn't know. Andrea knew and she was still with you, and I forgave her."

"Thank you for that." Emily could tell that Calvin was looking at Lily's as he said this.

"Why don't you go sit next to her?"

"I don't think she wants me to sit next to her."

"No, I think she does," Emily said, and Calvin Bruno stood up and went to sit next to Lily. She didn't react or push him away — she didn't even look at him. They both sat there next to one another in the same pew. After Calvin Bruno stood up to sit next to Lily, Samantha Little stood up to sit next to Albert. Emily looked back and saw them sitting next to each other as Samantha held Albert's hand while Albert sat crying. Emily stood up to sit next to Detective Stevenson, her biological mother, and her foster mother. The priest went on with Andrea's eulogy. The memorial lasted thirty more minutes, and then everyone who came by left the church. Emily and Detective Stevenson stood on the steps.

"Detective Stevenson, I'll drop my mom back off. We're having food at Mama Kim's house. You want to come?"

"No, I gotta catch a plane to Alabama to see my folks. My dad is having a retirement party."

"That's great. I'm glad you're going to see them."

"Yeah, me too. Thank you for pushing me to do so."

"You're welcome. I just wanted to let you know, I dropped out of school yesterday and signed up for the police academy." Emily smiled as she told Detective Stevenson her good news.

"That's great, I'm sure you'll do well and you'll be an officer before you know it. I'm really proud of you Emily."

"I'm proud of you too," Emily hugged Detective Stevenson. As she hugged her Emily noticed a very attractive man standing by Detective Stevenson's car. "Is that your boyfriend?"

"Yeah, that's him." Detective Stevenson waved at him and smiled.

"Dr. Brooks?" Detective Williams said, as he noticed Detective Stevenson's boyfriend standing next to her car. "Stevie, your man is Dr. Brooks?" he asked as he walked down the stairs to shake his hand.

"Evan was the doctor that removed a bullet from Willie last year," Detective Stevenson explained to Emily.

"Nice, and good looking too. You take care, and tell your family I said hello."

"I will." Detective Stevenson walked down the steps and got into the car with Dr. Brooks. They started their drive to the airport as Emily drove with Andrea's urn in the passenger seat to Mama Kim's house.

"Me and you, sis, always," Emily said to the urn that she buckled in the passenger seat as she drove off.

About the Author

Prior to becoming an author, writer, publisher, and doctor of early childhood education, Dr. Ariel Sylvester, Ed.D. guided and taught children in many capacities in public and private sectors in Chicago, Illinois where she was born and raised. She was an after school care teacher, summer camp teacher, apprentice teacher, substitute teacher, temporary assigned teacher, and full-time teacher. Her longest teacher role was a 2nd grade teacher with Chicago Public Schools at a school that she previously attended as a child. Ariel is also an activist for single-mother college students and helping them complete their collegiate degrees. She has ambitious goals of helping them to break poverty cycles and create educational attainment cycles for them and their children. She is also the sole proprietor of Pretty Nerd Publishing. If you enjoyed this book, please read some of her other books listed on her publishing company's website prettynerdpublishing.com.

www.ingramcontent.com/pod-product-compliance
Ingram Content Group UK Ltd.
Pitfield, Milton Keynes, MK11 3LW, UK
UKHW012155240726
13966UKWH00002B/348

9 781958 240281